HOLLOW DAZE

HOLLOW DAZE

ODIE HAWKINS

iUniverse LLC
Bloomington

HOLLOW DAZE

iUniverse books may be ordered through booksellers or by contacting:

iUniverse LLC
1663 Liberty Drive
Bloomington, IN 47403
www.iuniverse.com
1-800-Authors (1-800-288-4677)

Cover art by: Tony Gleeson, www.tonygleeson.com

Cover design by iUniverse Design Team

Author's Photo by
Zola Salena-Hawkins
www.flickr.com/photos/32886903@N02

ISBN: 978-1-4917-0660-2 (sc)
ISBN: 978-1-4917-0661-9 (ebk)

Library of Congress Control Number: 2013916532

Printed in the United States of America

iUniverse rev. date: 09/18/2013

CONTENTS

Dedicated to all those who went through the

"Hollow Daze".

CHAPTER 1

An Evening with My Hoes by Icepick Slim

I had been promising my hoes a night on the town for the past three months. It had reached the point where Lulu, my bottom, had started dropping real serious hints about the situation.

"Uh, Daddy, remember what you said about us havin' a night out with you?" she'd ask.

I didn't have a serious problem with the idea of taking my hoes off the track for a "date." The problem was one that they had created themselves. They were making so much money for me it was hard to even think about stopping that cash flow, even for one night.

Lulu, Paula, Clarrisa, Margo, Tanisha, and Sammye (my bi girl) were money magnets. All I had to do was just drop them on the track and come back two or three hours later, and they would rain money down on me.

I was addicted to money, and they knew that—they catered to that in order to keep me in a good mood. They also knew I was an evil ass motherfucker when I didn't get my "fix" every day. Some pimps—I'm not going to name names—get off into underhanded shit about their pimpin'. I've never been into subterfuges and shit. I've always been straight up; I pimped for the adrenaline rush that those greenbacks gave me. I think I must be one of the few men on the planet who could get an erection by having enough hundred dollar bills piled in my lap. I could get aroused just looking at a stack of Benjamins, but my man would really come up for a pile in my lap.

Okay, so I had promised my sextet a night out. I worked out an agenda that would have something for everybody. I knew Lulu and Paula wanted some Thai food, so I made a note to call for reservations at the Sompun on Saturday at midnight. That was one of the great things about the Sompun, other than the food—they stayed open 'til four o'clock in the morning on Saturdays.

Clarrisa, Margo, and Tanisha wanted to hear some live music of some kind and then shake their asses a li'l bit. And Sammye, my bi girl, was down for everything.

I wasn't a heavy coke user, and I didn't encourage a lot of chemical drug use. One of my mentors from long ago, Big Al, once told me, "Keep that chemical shit at arm's distance from you and your stable. If anybody starts snortin' anything or shootin' anything on a regular basis, it will shred your whole program to cat shit. Take my word for it—been there, done that, got the T-shirt."

But this was a special occasion, and I knew my hoes would enjoy getting high with their man. I put in a call to Mr. Dandy Candy, a dude who got his stuff straight from the mountains of Bolivia. He had a boutique operation going on.

"I don't need to be peddling five tons of blow every week or any of that crazy shit. Between me and my contact in Bolivia, I can bring in enough money to do whatever I want to do. And that's what it's all about, ain't it? Doing whatever you want to do."

I had a few philosophical differences of opinion with Mr. Dandy Candy, 'specially about the money thang. I could never really understand why he could be content to simply pull in a few grand every day. My feeling was that I would try to make a mint every time I had the chance.

Remember, dope has a self-refueling market. So why didn't I throw my hat in the coke ring? Well, I guess I could use three natural excuses. Number one, there was always an element of danger on the fringes of the drug scene. Pick up any daily paper, and the first thing you come across is a piece about "a drug deal gone sour," meaning somebody just got his ass blown off—bad news.

Number two, I know enough about my addictive urges to know that I would be quite likely to snort up my profits.

Number three, pimpin' came natural to me; it was like something that had been blessed upon me. I had the magic necessary to turn

Mother Teresa out if she were alive and I had the chance to run my game down on her.

Anyway, I put in a three-grand order from Mr. Dandy.

"When do you want it?" he asked.

"Today is Wednesday, how about Saturday?"

"No problem, Icepick, no problem. Sounds like you getting ready to do a li'l partayin'."

"Yeah, Dandy, I decided to give my hoes a night on the town," I told him.

"Wow! You actually givin' them a whole evenin' off?"

"They've earned it, Dandy. Believe me—they've earned it."

"What time Saturday?"

"How about high noon?"

"High noon—ha-ha. I like that. The courier will be there at high noon—ha-ha."

"Later, Dandy."

"Yeah, be cool, Icepick."

Thursday and Friday, the two days leading up to our Saturday night out, were filled with tension and drippin' drama. It was definitely the excitement building up that caused Lulu and Paula to get at each other. It was no profound secret that Paula wanted Lulu's privileged position. It was also no profound secret that Lulu held her privileged position in the scheme of things by virtue of being consistently the biggest earner in our house.

"Paula, let's get something straight again," I said. "Each one of you all is where you are because that's the position you've earned. Now, let's cut this cat scratchin' 'n' shit out. Understand what I'm sayin' to you, Paula?"

"Yes, Daddy, I understand but . . ."

"If you understand what I'm sayin', then you know there's no room for buts."

I had to come down real cold on Paula because she was real fine, and she knew it. She was beige-yellow, had almond-shaped green eyes and fly-back hair, and was stacked like a brick shithouse.

Lulu was fine in her own right; dark chocolate, gorgeous body, filled with piss 'n' vinegar, but she didn't stop traffic the way Paula stopped traffic. That was the catch for Paula; she just couldn't figure out how it was that Lulu could bring in more than she did. I was a little puzzled myself until Lulu explained it to me.

"I think it's like this, Daddy, if you don't mind me sayin' this?"

I nodded my permission. Shit, if a hoe could bring in two or three thousand a night, not even working all night, she definitely had my permission to speak.

"I think Paula has this attitude about herself, like she thinks she's too good to be doin' this. I think she sorta half steps sometimes because of her attitude. Now me, I know I'm a hoe, and I want to be the best hoe Daddy ever had."

See why Lulu was my bottom—my number one? 'Cause she was a warrior-hoe. I used to pay close attention to the way my hoes prepared to get out there and do battle, in a manner of speaking, with the other hoes. Lulu knew how to dress to bring out her best features—how to wear just the right kind of earrings, the right kind of perfume. "My momma once told me that there are basically only two kinds of perfume a woman should wear," she explained. "Funk from her own funky ass and Chanel N°5. I prefer Chanel N°5."

Paula, on the other hand, might just put on damned near anything damned near if I didn't watch her. I had to make her change clothes on more than one occasion, because she was getting ready to get out there in blue jeans with holes in the knees. And pin curlers in her hair. Can you imagine? I went off on her ass.

I had developed a special way of going off. When my voice got real low and this icy calm settled over me, everybody knew that I was just about a finger snap away from sticking my foot up somebody's ass.

"Paula, look, you can't even think about going outta here, representing me, wearing no such shit as that," I'd tell her. "We are a class act, no matter where we are."

And it was true, we *were* a class act. It took me damned near two hours to get dressed every evening I hit the streets. I had to have my hair done once a week, had to have that apricot-cucumber facial every other week, frequent manicures *and* pedicures, the whole shebang. Clothes? I used to change complete outfits twice a day if I felt like it. And both of my rides—I had an ol'-fashioned Jag and a Benz that had to be sparkling and shining like new money when I pulled out of the garage.

That's the front I maintained, and here is Paula, trying to look like a bohemian or whatever. I wouldn't have it. No matter whether my hoes were strolling the track or keeping a date at the Rockefeller Plaza Hotel, they had to be looking good and acting good.

Here, take a look at this while I'm on the subject. I got six bona fide hoes—yes, even including Paula with her wayward ass—and I have to deal with them, I have to have their respect, and they have to do what they have to do for me. It's not about me taking from them; it's about them giving to me, and I must be careful to keep the foundation for that state of affairs in place. It's a delicate balancing act and demands a lot of psychological understanding. And you have to remember that the same thing does not work for everybody.

Hoes are not all alike. Some people might have the mistaken notion that hoes are basically some downtrodden, low-self-esteem dum-dums who have been led astray by some fast-talking flimflam man. Now, to be honest and objective about the scene, I have to admit that those types of people do exist, without a doubt. But I'm not talking about them. I'm talking about a different breed altogether. I'm talking about some intelligent, resourceful, quick-thinking females, like Lulu, Paula, Clarissa, Margo, Tanisha, and Sammye— my hoes.

One must be careful about stereotyping hoes. Before I managed to become involved with this particular sextet, remember they asked me to pimp them. I didn't beg to become their man—dig it? Before I became involved with my current people, I had the misfortune of establishing a household with eight rebel hoes. It's a shame that I have to admit this, but I had cobbled together the worst kind of ensemble. Every hoe in the house had issues and was rebellious to boot.

Well, maybe it had something to do with my youth; I was only twenty-three at the time, and my knowledge of hoe psychology still left a lot to be desired. They were bringing in the dough, but they were also skimming, lying, conniving, and rebelling.

It reached the point where I had to go to sleep with my Luger under my pillow—whenever I did get a chance to sleep. There was always some shit going on. It got to the point where I was on the verge of becoming a gorilla pimp. I would spend damned near a whole week cracking people upside the head, putting my foot up somebody's ass, or whipping somebody's ass with my big leather belt. And then I would have to start the week off all over again.

I had to talk with my mentor, Big Al, about the situation. "Pick, from the description you just gave me, I'd have to say that you have wound up with a stable full of rebels. Now here is what you can do about that: you can either tame the wild beasts, or you can put 'em back out there in the jungle."

"How would I tame them?" I asked.

"Just keep on doin' what you're doin', but I don't see that as a long-term solution. And at the end of the day, it might do you more harm than it would do them. What I mean by that is that you might become calloused, cold, cruel, mean, evil. The other solution, like I said, is to put 'em back out there in the jungle."

"What would you do, Big Al?"

"I'd kick their asses real good one last time, just so they would retain that memory, and then I would release 'em—one by one. Remember, Pick, the planet is loaded with potential hoes, would-be hoes, bona fide hoes. I don't think you ought to subject yourself to this kind of abuse. I'm just lookin' at these raccoon rings around your eyes . . . . I bet you haven't had a good night's sleep in weeks."

"You got that right. Thanks, Big Al. I know what to do now."

It took me approximately six weeks to push, kick, beat, and knock those rebel hoes away from me. Rebel-like, they resisted my efforts, but I won. I had to. Ever seen a defeated pimp? He's a sad ass sight. I can tell you that. Some of them get beaten down so bad they wind up looking like hunchbacks.

As I pushed one away, I replaced her with another, better type. So I wound up with this current sextet. I can't say I got lucky; I got smarter.

CHAPTER 2

Girls' Night

Damn, you would've thought that they were going to their high school prom or something. No matter what, business had to come first. I kept everybody out there for four extra hours, just to halfway cover for what was going to be lost on Saturday night. I think I did them a favor, because their energy level was so high that they might've done something stoopid; they didn't know what to do with themselves. Clarissa and Margo got busted an hour before closing time. *Damn.*

We had those two cops—one Black, the other one White, whom we had nicknamed "Blackie" and "Whitey"—who just loved to mess with people. They knew my stable on sight, and they just loved to annoy us. The bust was no biggie; I was down at the station to bail Clarissa and Margo out within the hour. What would it mean? Basically nothing. The bust was an occupational hazard for a hoe, and they usually took it in stride—a simple misdemeanor fine.

On this occasion, when I led Clarissa and Margo down to the Jag, they were hyperventilating or some shit.

"Hey, y'all, calm down. What the hell is wrong with you?" I asked. "Did you think I wasn't coming to bail you out?"

Margo spoke for both of them. "Oh, we knew you were coming, Daddy; we knew that. We were just concerned about the possibility of something happenin'—somethin' that would prevent us from keepin' our date tomorrow."

I had to smile. Nothing like an excited hoe.

Saturday morning I slept till about eleven thirty, when Tanisha and Sammye bought me a couple of pieces of French toast and a snifter of my favorite cognac—Arc de Triomphe. Let those other fools suck on that Hennessey. Courvoisier and Martel, Arc de Triomphe was my thing.

The really nice thing about being self-employed is that you can set your own schedule. I didn't ease out of bed until I heard the bling-bling chimes signaling the arrival of Mr. Dandy Candy's courier.

"I'll get that," I called out from my bedroom, surprising everybody, because they knew I never answered the door or anything like that. I slipped my black silk robe on over my black silk pajama bottoms, counted three grand plus two hundred out of my bedside table drawer, and strolled to the door.

"Yes?" I asked into the intercom. Our condo had maximum security—no strays allowed.

"Candy," this real sultry female voice replied. I buzzed to let the sultry voice in, looking out of the corner of my eye at my crew. They were pretending not to pay any attention to me and weren't doing a good job of it. I compounded their interest by stepping out into the vestibule to meet Mr. Candy's "deliveryman."

Candy had done it again. This time he had sent over a Spanish-looking woman—spectacularly fine. She looked like a cross between that ol' Italian movie star Sophia Loren and the beautiful African-American actress Halle Berry. I didn't give her any kind of square ass up-'n'-down look, but I let her know, via my vibe, that I liked her looks and that she would be welcome to join my stable on any given day. There's an awful lot you can say with an eyebrow and a half smile.

"Uh, how much do I owe you?" I asked.

"My name is Jo Gu, and that will be three thou."

I counted three thousand two hundred into her well-manicured right hand. She handed me a small glassine baggie and recounted the money.

"I think you have overpaid, sir."

"No, I haven't. The two hundred is for you. You might want to buy yourself an ice cream cone or something."

"Well, thank you and have a good day." She seemed genuinely pleased with my li'l tip. I stood with my hands jammed into the dressing gown pockets, staring at her as she waited for the elevator. I imagined her measurements were 38-24-36—something like that— and brimming over with class.

"Uh, Jo Gu, how is it?" I asked before she left.

"It's pharmaceutical," she answered with a shy little smile. I felt that a live one was escaping, but I didn't want to act anxious about it. After all, she might be Mr. Candy's private stock.

"Jo Gu, I'm going to have a li'l thing next month, think you'd like to make it?"

"Definitely."

I liked that, she wasn't a gabber. "How will I get in touch with you?" I asked.

She strolled back over with a card in her hand just as the elevator came. "You can reach me at one of these numbers."

"I'll be in touch."

"I'll look forward to it." And then she was gone, swallowed up by the elevator, leaving this tantalizing scent behind. I strolled back into the condo feeling as though I had accomplished something. Everybody in the place knew better than to be throwing questions at me about anything. I would open up when I opened up and not a second before.

The place was beehive busy; Tanisha and Sammye were doing each other's feet and nails, while Margo was pressing something out on the ironing board. Clarrisa and Paula had laid about thirty outfits, with matching accessories, out on their beds, trying to decide what they were going to wear. Lulu was sewing something. It was a few minutes after noon, and my hoes were preparing themselves to have a date with their man.

I eased into the upstairs bathroom, tapped a couple of lines of the blow on somebody's compact mirror and tooted up. It only took two snorts for me to determine that I *did* have some pharmaceutical-quality cocaine. That ice-cold burn up my nose, followed by the frontal lobe face-freeze said it all.

I made a mental note to call Mr. Dandy Candy and give him a *thumbs-up* for his product. Like I said earlier, I wasn't too heavily into chemical intoxication, given the kind of advice I had been given by my godfather *and* mentor, Big Al.

"Look at it this, Pick, if a funky chump can't get up on a li'l herb and some fire water, then we know for damned certain the minute he strolls up that chemical path, his ass is in serious trouble. Chemicals? Cocaine, *heron*, pills—chemicals. Personally, I believe that a whole bunch of these chemicals were thrown on the table in front of the Black pimp to keep us from pimpin' correctly. Hey, let's face it, if you wind up with a funky chump who is more in love with a white powder than anything else on the planet, then what's that? That's fucked up—that's what that is."

I didn't often stray too far away from Big Al's counseling, but this was, after all, a special occasion. I was taking my sextet out. French toast, Arc de Triomphe, and pharmaceutical-quality coke—I was ready.

"Lulu, call up that limo service and have them pick us up around eight," I instructed. "Be sure and tell them *not* to send one of those big ol' long, ugly ass things. We want a black, classy vehicle that will seat seven—with a bar. We don't need any TV or anything like that. Get at that!

Paula, Clarissa, Margo, what're y'all doing?"

They damned near fell over themselves trying to explain what they were doing. I didn't listen; I didn't really care. I was totally wired after two thick lines of cocaine from Bolivia, and I felt powerful. I had made an instant decision to do two things: number one, hide a portion of this superior blow in my top drawer; number two, don't turn my crew on till a half hour or so before we get ready to go out. The last thing I needed was to spend a whole day surrounded by six wired up hoes.

It was a funny day, now that I think back on it. I made several little pit stops in the bathroom during the course of the day, reinforcing all the macho elements of my nature. I came out of the bathroom at one point, saw everybody lounging around and watching TV, and the first weird thought that came to my mind was, *What're these hoes doing, sitting around on their asses doing nothing?!* But then I had to remember—I gave them some time off. I made a silent decision to not do that again. It really unnerved me to see them lounging around, being unproductive.

'Round about six o'clock, Sammye and Tanisha made some tuna on rye sandwiches. Only a couple of people nibbled on them; they were saving their appetites for the dinner we were going to have at the Sompun Thai restaurant. But we were on the third bottle of Arc de Triomphe.

It was 7:15 on the nose when I lined everybody up at the dining room table. I can still see their mascaraed eyes pop out when I tapped the first two lines on the mahogany ebony table.

"Lulu?" I called out.

I gave my bottom the rolled up hundred dollar bill for first toots, then Paula, Clarissa, Margo, Tanisha, and finally Sammye. And then I did my thing and rotated them for seconds. By the time the limo came, we were all in a state of grace. Sammye hugged me on the way out. "Oh, Daddy, you so good to us."

I nodded in agreement. I gave Lulu what I had left in the glassine bag to hide in one of her private places. This was a woman who could conceal razor blades in her mouth, so hiding a little cocaine was no problem. It was a substantial amount, even after I had hidden my secret share. That was the nice thing about Mr. Candy; he always gave you a good bag.

I was going to "line us up" from time to time as the evening went on, just to keep everybody properly elevated.

CHAPTER 3

Party Time

The people at the Sompun Thai restaurant loved to see us coming. They knew they had their day's, maybe their week's, money made when we sat down. The Sompun was designed to look like somebody's pad. It was large enough to sit fifty people, with the kitchen right in the center and tables arranged in a circular pattern around the kitchen.

It was a lively spot. On two occasions, we had witnessed fistfights between two chefs. We never found out what it was all about because the maître d' stonewalled us.

"Mr. Sompun, what was that all about?" I had asked him.

"What, sir?"

"Those two chefs trying to beat the shit out of each other with their spatulas."

"Can I bring you another Singha, sir?" the maître d' questioned.

That's the way they did it; they were cool. It was the kind of place that maintained a very high standard—both with food and otherwise. I lost count of the number of times I had eaten there, whether by my lonesome, with a couple of numbers of my crew, or the whole entourage, and right there at the next table would be Miss Whatsher Name or Mr. Whatshis Name. But nobody made a big thang out of the fact that Miss Whateverher Name or Mr. Whateverhis Name was there.

I'm damned sure a whole lot of people wanted to know who we were on that Saturday evening I gave my hoes the night off. First off, we eased out of this limo right in front of the place—Lulu, Paula, Clarissa, Margo, Tanisha, Sammye, and me, all of us loaded on Mr. Dandy Candy's superior merchandise.

For those who haven't tried it, I just got to recommend Arc de Triomphe cognac and unstomped on Bolivian cocaine if you want to really be cool. We had done a couple of lines each just before we exited from the limo—the kind of shit that gives you that edge to your hipness.

It was a crowded restaurant that night. I don't know who they thought we were when we made our entrance, but they damned sure knew we were out there.

Let's start with Lulu—check it out. Lulu had this cornrow thing on her head that looked like a Cedric Adams drawing. She was wearing this blue dress with white piping running along the fringes that looked like Arabic writing, formfitting over her curves like it was molded to her fine ass. I saw a couple of White boys stab themselves in the face with their chopsticks staring at her as she snake-walked to our centerpiece table, right there in front of the entrance to the Sompun Thai kitchen.

Paula had that cold thang about her when she was high, like she was saying, "Hey, I know I'm the finest yaller bitch y'all have ever seen, but my heart belongs to Daddy." And she had taken my advice and wore her skin-tight Vietnamese black pajama outfit. The thing was so tight on her ass that you could see the split in her stuff with no effort at all.

Clarissa had one of those African asses that challenged the connoisseur to hold it in both hands. There were only five brothers in the place, three of them with White girls, but you could sense their urge to grab hold of Clarissa's ass—well, some of it anyway. And being the super hoe she was, she didn't let anybody off the hook by strolling to our table, indicating with each measured, swiveling step that this was the ass they wanted to fondle, caress, hold, cum onto, pay for.

Margo was a belly dancer, and she knew how to convey that with a simple walk across the space of a crowded Thai restaurant. Her stuff was definitely helped by her half midriff gown, with the veils swirling all around her body.

Tanisha was damned near buck fuckin' nekid! You know how hot it is with some of these women who have almost perfect dimensions and are exhibitionists to boot. It was like she had draped some see-through gauze around three postage stamps—one down there and two up there. And Sammye was right there in the front line with her see-through T-shirt and her 38C cups dancing upright and this Bolivian coke-caused look on her face that said, "we bad."

Me? When Sammye helped me peel the red, silk-lined black cape off of my red-and-black pinstriped suit, I could see more than a few people on the verge of applauding.

I could understand their emotional reaction—I really could—but it wasn't about them; it was about my night out with my hoes. Maybe it was my imagination, but it seemed like the Sompun restaurant had frozen itself into place, become the backdrop for our act.

They all ordered their favorite things, lubricated by that beautiful little Thai beer—Singha. I had four flasks of Arc de Triomphe with me, so I didn't fool around with the beer. I knew I would be sick as a dog if I tried to mix my stuff. It was a gorgeous two hours, really gorgeous. We sat there, feasting on those incredible Thai dishes. (How in the hell do you stuff chicken wings?) And laughing and joking about all kinds of shit. I had to put a damper on things only twice, when Sammye and Tanisha tried to pull off a couple of antipimp jokes. No, I signaled with a down turn of my left eyebrow, *I will not sit here and listen to antipimp jokes. We go through too much shit with you hoes to have y'all make fun of us; no jokes about our relationship.*

Other than that, we had a damned good dinnertime. All of them were hungry, so we ate like a king and queens—as much as we wanted. What was the check? Four or five hundred dollars? Something like that. It didn't matter; the important thing for me was that everybody would be happy, because the following day, Sunday, they were going to be back on the job, making up for lost revenue.

I thought some of the people in the restaurant were going to applaud as we made our exit. It was quite obvious, as squares, that they had no idea who we really were or where we were coming from. We popped back into the limo, and I laid out a couple of lines for everybody. My hoes were in an adoration state. I had fed them well, I had given them lines of superior Bolivian cocaine, and I hadn't been forced to abuse anybody. What more could a real hoe want? Off we went to the De WaWa Club.

"Oh, Daddy, could we go to the De WaWa Club? That's where everybody goes!"

"Reservations have already been made," I told them.

"Oh, Daddy, you think of everything!"

I *didn't* think of everything. I had to scramble through a few calls and a few contacts to get us seats at the De WaWa Club. Yeah, I knew it was supposed to be where all the hip and the semihip (the "playas") gathered, but it didn't mean skippy to me. From all I knew about the scene, it was supposed to show where your rankings were in the game, or some such foolishness as all that.

That really troubled me, like pimpin' could be done by Gallup polls or something. Once again, I had to go to my mentor, Big Al, about an understanding of the situation.

"Don't pay that PR/crazy shit no attention, Pick. You can't measure good pimpin' by polls or parties," Big Al explained. "Spiritually speakin', you can have a pimp who is doin' excellent pimpin', but he won't have the visibility of a funky chump who is doin' jive-ass pimpin'. It's got a lot to do with the kinds of perceptions people have. Most of us have been taught that numbers tell the story, and that's where we go. That's not always true.

"Think about it. We've had a number of revolutions happen on this Earth, with only a few people doin' it; think about Marx, Castro, Mao, and a whole bunch of others. They didn't have the numbers at first, because their cause wasn't popular. Think about Obama when he first kicked off. There were a whole bunch of African-Americans who didn't support him for a whole bunch of reasons—and a whole bunch of Whites too.

"I think, number one, they thought he was going to be assassinated. Number two, they had to sit back and see if he was going to get White support. And all the rest of those other weirdass factors. But at the end of the day, he pulled it off."

The De WaWa club—first off, you had to be "somebody" to get in. That meant that you were willing to give this mountain of a man guarding the entrance a hundred-dollar tip. I had given him so many hundred-dollar tips he knew me and my crew.

"Evenin' Mr. Slim, ladies, your table has been reserved." Man Mountain knew that I didn't like being down front, in the first or second row of tables where all of the wannabes, the would-bes, the has-beens, and the squares were seated. I had learned from experience that the stage side tables were too close to the action. If they had a dance group, for example, the dancers would damned near be stepping in your drink. And if there was an instrumental group, the up close sound system would blow your ear drums out.

Our reserved table in this airplane hangar-sized place was over to the left where we could see and be seen. It took about five minutes after our drinks were served before people started doing that. "Look, there's Icepick Slim and his hos," I heard them start to whisper.

My hoes loved the attention. They primped and preened, being a bit full of themselves because they were out with me. A Brazilian group was playing on this particular night, and they were hot! And I really mean *hot*! They even had me out on the dance floor, shaking my booty with the rest of them for a few minutes. And everybody knew I wasn't the booty-shaking type.

The management did a clever thing; right after twenty hot minutes of samba, they rotated a very cool five-piece jazz ensemble onto the stage to give us a chance to rest.

"The Brazilian Dance and Drum Ensemble will return later in the program," the MC announced. That was the way they did it at the De WaWa Club, going from one type of music to another. It might be a signer one time, a jazz trio, a hip-hop rapper and friends, some Afro-Cuban stuff, whatever.

My crew was having a good time, and that was all that mattered. I think it was my mentor, Big Al, who once said, "Keep your hoes happy; a happy hoe is a productive hoe."

Lulu was the one who pulled my coat, as usual.

"Daddy, Paula been gone to the ladies for a long time. You want me to go and see if she's sick or something?" she asked.

"Uh, yeah, go check her out."

Lulu came wading back through the crowd about ten minutes later with a funny look on her face.

"Where's Paula? She okay?"

I could tell from the way she answered that everything was *not okay*.

"Uh, she's okay; she's talkin' with somebody."

I didn't jump out of my seat and run to the ladies room. I cooled myself out for a few minutes before I made my move.

It took about ten minutes to get from our table to the back area of the club where the Men's and Women's room were located. I took the whole scene in at a glance. Paula was trying to get around this roadblock named Philly Joe Phil. I knew him by reputation. He was a pimp, well known for his gorilla-like mannerisms. He seemed to think he could go gorilla on any woman he came across.

Paula glanced up at me as though J.C. himself had arrived. I didn't waste a mumblin' word; I knew what had to be done, and I did it. I coldcocked Mr. Philly Joe Phil with a left to his right temple. He was a fairly big dude, about two hundred or so to my one hundred and seventy-five, but my left hook neutralized his weight advantage.

Philly Joe slumped down against the wall like a sack of wet clothes. I had hit a lot of people in my day, but he was my first knockout.

Mr. Man Mountain eased onto the scene like a giant shadow. "Uh, no problem, Mr. Slim. I was monitoring the situation, and I was about ten seconds away from intervening. But I see you took care of the matter. Mr. Phil was way outta line, and he paid the price. I don't have to tell you—we don't permit any form of misbehavior in the De WaWa Club. I'll see to it that Mr. Phil is off of the premises as soon as he comes to his senses. That was a sweet left hook you threw." And then he winked at me.

I knocked off a phony-ass military salute and stepped away from the scene with Paula clinging to my arm. You have to understand, I didn't left hook Phil because I was mad at him or anything. I coldcocked him because he was preventing one of my women from doing what she wanted to do. It was an object lesson in a way. If he could hold her up in the De WaWa Club, then he might feel privileged to do the same thing if he ran into her in the streets. I put a stop to that possibility right on the spot.

Paula couldn't wait to get back to our table to tell the others how I had knocked Phil out. "Daddy looked like Mohammed Ali when he hit him."

A few minutes later, Mr. Man Mountain escorted Phil out of the club, looking a li'l bit loopy legged. I made a silent vow to get back into the gym a little more often. What next?

"Let's go on over to Livin' Swell's place."

"*Oh yes, Livin' Swell!*"

"*Livin' Swell! Oh yes!*"

We made a hit coming in, and we made a hit going out. Who could miss me and six gorgeous women trippin' out to our waiting limo?

Off to "*Livin' Swell's*" place. "*Livin' Swell*" was what we all called this brother who owned this estate out there on the far south side. The place was huge, walled in like a castle, and you had to drive over a drawbridge to get onto the estate. *Livin' Swell's* real name was Percy Evans, but everybody called him *Livin' Swell* 'cause that's what he called himself.

"I'm livin' swell—that's why I call myself *Livin' Swell*," he'd say.

There were a whole bunch of rumors about how Livin' Swell came into his money; some folks said that he had inherited a few million and built on that. Somebody else said that he had won the lottery. And of course, somebody else said that he had made his money dealing drugs. He could've done all of those things, or maybe he had done none of them. It didn't really matter all that much; the important thing was that he was livin' swell.

We might've been semiresponsible for him being able to sponsor a lush lifestyle too. Spending an evening at Livin' Swell's pad cost some money. It cost two hundred bucks to park your ride and walk inside—that's two hundred dollars per couple. He would give me a li'l discount for my six, but everything else was cash on the barrelhead.

There was coke from the resident coke dealer if you had a yen for that. We didn't need any cocaine; we had our own. The lines were getting thinner, but we had enough. The four or five bars scattered around the mansion had the best liquor you could drink. They even had Arc de Triomphe.

"Lookahere, Swell, if you want me to keep coming up in here, you got to stock something I like," I'd told him awhile back.

So that's how we wound up with Arc de Triomphe at three of the bars. But aside from all of that, the brother provided the "spoiled people"—someone once called us the "ghetto jet set"—with a really hip atmosphere. If you wanted to go swimming at four o'clock in the morning, he had swimming gear and *two* life guards on duty at this Olympic-sized pool on the roof. On the roof! Can you get ready for that?

Never been to Hughgo Boy Hefner's mansion in Chicago or California, but I'm sure it couldn't hold a torch to Livin' Swell's stuff. Big, high-ceiling rooms on three floors with something happening on each floor. There might be a dance band, somebody performing, a comedy act, or whatever in the first floor ballroom.

On one occasion, at about dawn, he had a couple of tango dancers do their thang. It was absolutely tantalizing.

Everything was beautifully furnished and tasteful—nothing plastic or glitzy. You could get breakfast if you wanted it or enjoy a private screening of a gorgeous, old-fashioned porno film—the kind they used to do without condoms. The place was sizzling.

Every now and then *Livin' Swell* would slide through to make sure that everybody and everything was cool. "How're y'all doin'? Everything swell?" he asked.

"Oh yes, Livin' Swell," I assured him, "everything is fine. All we need now is a li'l breakfast."

"You guys wanna eat here or come down to the dinin' room?"

"We'll come down to the dining room."

It was about six o'clock; dawn was creeping in on us as we made our way down to the dining room. I exchanged greetings with a couple of my fellow pimps. It seemed that we were the only ones who could really stay up all night and enjoy the scene at *Livin' Swell's* place.

They had those lacy little crêpes suzette that Swell's Vietnamese chef made. I had a short stack with a cup of black coffee. My crew ate like a sextet of lumberjacks. They were obviously in an indulgent mood.

After breakfast, there was nothing to do but wrap it up and call it a night. We eased back into the limo and woke the driver up. Poor guy—his ass was dragging.

"Let's take a little stroll on the lakefront before we call it a night."

The cocaine lines were even thinner now, but we still had some—just enough to toot us over to the lake. I can still see the looks the early-morning joggers gave us—this dude with his cape on and six gorgeous women trailing along behind him.

Back in the limo, Lulu spoke for the crew when she kissed me on the side of face and said, "Thank you, Daddy. Thank you for a beautiful night out."

"Let's see how things go. We might take a little cruise to Jamaica or somewhere in the fall, depending on what happens," I teased.

They got all wired up about that. What the hell, it was June. If they worked hard and well, we could definitely afford to go anywhere we wanted to go a few months from now.

They were beginning to look a little bent by the time we got back to the pad.

"Awright y'all, I want everybody to sleep a few hours," I announced. "We want to be back out there takin' care business at one o'clock this afternoon."

They all nodded in agreement. Nobody could complain about anything. I had just given my hoes a night off.

CHAPTER 4

Dirty Hollow

Benton Marsh, the owner, publisher, and CEO of Hollow Daze Publishing House Company stared at the small pile of blue-covered contracts on his uncluttered desk. A contract for Icepick Slim's book, *Pimpin'*. A contract for Ronald Cummins's *Daddy Smooth*. A contract for Jack Mozel's latest, *Death Time. My God, how many books has this guy written for us?* Benton thought.

A contract for the Dawkin's book, *Time Out*. A contract for Ruuth Morrissey's bio of Zora Neal Hurston and Alice W. Hiker's sexy new novel, *Open Sesame*.

He leaned back in his faded-brown, leather chair. *Damn! These new dentures are a pain in the ass.* He removed his uppers and lowers and stared at them for a few minutes. *Wonder what I would look like without those things?*

There was no need to go beyond the last time he had considered the thought as he looked at himself in his morning-shaving mirror. Cheeks sunken, hair dye job fading, arthritis kicking in and forcing him to bend over—he looked twenty years older than his real age of sixty.

He carefully repositioned his uppers and lowers. I can grow older later; now is the time to stay as young as I can, for as long as I can. There's money to be made. A soft tapping on the door of his office took him away from his self-absorption.

"Yes, come in," he called.

The gaunt face of his editor, Clay Block, peeked around the corner of the door. "You wanted to see me, Benton?"

"Yeah, Clay, come on in and sit. I want to talk to you about these new books." *The guy looks like death warmed over*, Benton thought.

Benton wasn't well read, but he thought he knew a good book when he saw one, especially if he was backed up by Clay Block, his editor at Hollow Daze Publishing House for the past ten years. It didn't matter that Clay kept a fifth of Jack Daniels in the left hand drawer of his editor's desk, or even that Clay Block was gay. The only thing that really mattered was that Clay baby had dug into the Hollow Daze slush pile and pulled out five best-selling Black writers (Benton couldn't make any sense out of the term *African-American*) during the past six years. And one White woman who took great pride in tryin' to write "Black."

Benton Marsh thought her claim to fame was the result of an identity crisis, but her stuff was selling and that was all that mattered. Benton also thought of himself as a benevolent guy. "After all, if Hollow Daze hadn't decided to publish these people, they would still be unknown and unheard of," he always said.

He never bothered to remind his audiences that he and his partner, Ron Wildstock, were making huge profits from the sales of Hollow Daze's "Black Experience" line. And the Playboy magazine in ebony that Ron was enthused by/with, that he head titled "*Duh Playa.*"

"So let's hear it, Clay," Benton began. He watched Clay do a little wobbly stutter step to the chair in front of his desk. *How the hell does this guy get toasted at ten o'clock in the morning? What kind of day can follow that?*

"Well, Ben-ton," Clay Block started off in his whisky, gravelly Mississippi baritone, "where do you want me to start?"

"How about at the beginning, Clay? Seems like that would be a suitable starting point."

"I turned in synopses—"

"I know you did, Clay, and I've got 'em, but I wanted to get a live feeding. You know what I mean? Do you mind?"

Clay Block tented his well-manicured fingers together under his chin and stared into a far corner for a few moments, a habit that

Benton hated. He waited impatiently for his chief editor-dude to collect himself.

"Awright, well, let me start with Icepick Slim's *Pimpin'*. God!—Where in the world do these people find these names? You think his family name was Slim?"

"Okay, we don't give a shit what the monkey's name is," Benton snapped. "We just want to know if his or her shit will sell. Okay?"

Clay Block glanced at the blue-covered contracts on his boss's desk. *What point did it make to try to soft-pedal anything? he* wondered. "Here goes . . . the subject matter is raw and revolting. I find the whole idea of a man taking advantage of women despicable," Clay stated matter-of-factly.

"I think you've expressed your outrage sufficiently in your critique. So what about sales?"

"It seems to me that a certain class of Blacks would be interested in this kind of stuff. And some Whites too—the young ones."

"That's what I wanted to hear, Clay, we can save the moral outrage for another day. Let's go on—Ronald Cummins's *Daddy Smooth*?"

Clay Block pursed his lips. *Damn, I could use a drink*, he thought before beginning his review. "*Daddy Smooth*. Well, what can I say? It's ghetto, ghetto, ghetto. I supposed you could say it's 224 pages of ghetto violence, ghetto violence, and more ghetto violence."

Clay, the editor, did a mental flash drive review of *Daddy Smooth*.

"I want you to gobble up the tip end of this .357 Mag, bitch!"

"Awe c'mon, Daddy Smooth, I thought I was yo' nigga."

"You *was* my nigga, punk bitch!"

Bam! Bam! Bam!

"Damn, Smooth. Why did you have to blow the motherfucker's head off like that?"

"Why? I'll tell you why! When I got back here from Baghdad and found that this bitch-motherfucker-punk-ass dog had turned my sister, Ambrosia, out into them mean streets, I was determined to do something about it."

"But . . . but . . . what about all the sistas you done turned out, Smooth?"

"That's different. This was my baby sister."

"So now Kenyatta's homies is gonna come for yo' ass."

"I'm not afraid of them jive-ass motherfuckers! I am armed to the teeth and should be considered highly dangerous. My question to you is this: are you with me?"

"You know I got yo' back, Smooth. You know that."

"Uh-oh! Look out, there's one of Kenyatta's homies over there!"

Bam! Bam! Bam!

"Did you get him?"

"I think so. Let's go over to his bleedin' body on the street and find out."

They walk across the street, looking to the left and the right, all senses wired up. They look down at the body on the street with a big hole in his chest. He looked up at them, dying. But before his death, he said, "You shot me, Daddy Smooth. Why did you do that? I ain't had no beef with you."

"I . . . why did I do it? 'Cause if I didn't get you, you was gonna get me."

"For what?"

"'Cause I just shot your homie, Kenyatta."

"You killed Kenyatta?! Uh-oh, yo' ass is in serious trouble now."

"Nawww, it's yo' ass that's in serious trouble."

Bam! Bam! Bam!

"Damn! Smooth, you killed him."

"That's what usually happens when you shoot a motherfucker with a .357 Mag. Point-blank."

"So what do we do now?"

"I got some dynamite weed at my pad. Let's go get high."

"Why don't you walk in front of me. I don't wanna get my head blown off by accident."

"Why would I wanna blow your head off?"

"Well, I was just thinkin' maybe you was holdin' a grudge against me for what happened between me 'n' yo' momma whilst you was in Baghdad."

"What happened between you and my momma?"

"Okay, Clay," Benton interrupted. "You don't have to exhaust yourself. You're saying that Icepick's *Pimpin* is a piece of immoral trash, but it'll sell. Cummins's *Daddy Smooth* is a piece of ghetto violence that will sell. Jack Mozel has given us his usual formula pot sticker. How many books has that guy written for Hollow Daze?"

"About forty," Clay answered

"How the hell does this guy knock this stuff out so fast?"

"Well, I would imagine that generous toots of high-grade cocaine, plus a few fifths of Jack Daniels would definitely help the process."

"Really?" Benton questioned.

"I can't really say for sure, but we've had a whole bunch of writers turn out immense amounts of work while they were high on one thing or another."

Benton blinked, hardly able to believe his ears. *Hell, I'm not a writer, but I think it would be hard as hell to keep your thoughts together*, he thought. *How the hell could you keep your thoughts in any kind of order if you were plastered on cocaine and sour mash whiskey? I have a hard time staying awake after a dry martini or two.*

"Okay, so the guy sniffs cocaine, drinks a lotta Jack Daniels, and gives us a book every month," Benton finally said, breaking the silence. "What about this last one?"

Clay Block tented is fingers under his chin again.

Benton Marsh managed to conceal his disgust. *Why the hell did this guy have to go into some kind of trance every time you ask him about something?*

"Well, Ben-ton, let me start off by sayin' that *Death Time* is a typical Mozel piece. He gives us the typical story of a returning vet who decides to go up against the bad guys. He's a good guy in spite of the fact that he kills, tortures, mutilates, and does all of the other stuff that the bad guys do. Like I said, it's a typical Mozel piece.

"He's had vets returning from the First World War up to the latest war. As you know, Mozel is an Iraqi vet himself."

"No, I didn't know that," Benton noted. "You think *Death Time* will sell? We barely broke even on our last Mozel book. What the hell was it?"

"*The Death Squad.* And yes, I think that *Death Time* will go. That's my gut."

"Good. That leaves us with our two ladies—Ruuth Morrissey bio of Zora Neal Hurston and Alice W. Hiker's sexy novel, *Open Sesame*."

"I gotta say, the Morrison bio is a nice, solid read, but it may not sell too well."

"Why not?" Benton questioned.

Clay felt slightly antsy. How long were they going to go on? It was obvious that Benton was going to go with the books he was talking about. *Maybe he just wants to do this to annoy me*, Clay thought to himself.

"Why not? Well, it's hard for me to put it in words, but I sometimes get the feeling that Ruuth is trying too hard to be Black. I'm sure that most of her readers already know she's White. She could just relax and write and not try to be Black. Dig it?"

"Yeah, Clay, I understand all that. I'm asking you about the bottom line here. Do you think Ruuth Morrison's book will sell?"

"I'll have to be a li'l iffy about this one."

Benton shifted the Morrison contract to the bottom of the pile. *We'll see what the budget for advances looks like before we get to this one*, he thought. "That leaves as with Alice Hiker's *Open Sesame*," he noted.

"As usual, she's heavily into her sex bag. And as usual, her characters start screwin' from page one, and they keep on doin' it until the book comes to an end," Clay said.

"So?"

"So. Well, her last two books had the same basic format, and they sold well, so there's no reason to think that *Open Sesame* won't do well."

Benton Marsh stared at his editor; the editor stared back. They both stood up. The meeting was at an end. Benton had the information he wanted. Clay Block could get back to the job of editing material that he thought was way below his intellectual level and sipping coffee cups filled with Jack Daniels.

"Clay, forget about that punk-ass cognac, man, go for the gusto! Jack Daniels is a man's drink!" *Thank you, Jack Mozel, for steering me onto the path of Bourbon.*

"Clay, don't take an extraordinarily long lunch hour today. I may need to talk with you a little later."

Clay nodded politely, silently seething. *You asshole. You got nerve to want to tie me up with a bunch of congenital bullshit.*

"Hi, Clay, how's it goin'?"

"Oh hi, Carolyn. All is well, as in hell, all is well."

Block took casual notice of the receptionist carefully peeling stamps off of letters that hadn't been cancelled. *That cheap-ass bastard,* he thought.

CHAPTER 5

Hollow Operation

Benton Marsh eased out of his office to make a sneaky inspection of his staff. Carolyn was on the job, peeling stamps, answering the phones, and chomping on a wad of gum.

"Morning, Mr. Marsh," Carolyn called.

"Morning, Carolyn. Tell Mr. Wildstock I'd like to see him when he gets in."

"Oh, he's already here. He's in the photo section."

Benton stalked through the corridors, peeking into doorless offices. *I'm the only one who has a door here. Why should these people have doors on their offices? What're they trying to hide?*

He had to break up a little office chitchat between two secretaries. "Don't you people have any work to do?" But beyond that, the place was humming. Good.

In the photo section, Benton Marsh crept up behind his business partner, Ron Wildstock, as he used an old-fashioned magnifying glass to study the vaginal lips of the latest centerfold for *Duh Playa* magazine. *Duh Playa* was Wildstock's baby, a more colorful knock off of *Playboy* magazine. They were going into their tenth successful year of publishing Black crime fiction pulps and the raunchy *Playa*.

"Awe c'mon, Ron, you can't make me believe that Black men will buy a colored version of *Playboy*," Benton had told Ron.

"Bent, read my lips—niggas will buy anything if it's pushed properly."

28

"I can't support that, Ron."

"Sure you can. Just think about it—ten years ago when we first cobbled our coins together to start Hollow Daze Publishing, you didn't think it would be *the* spot for Black crime fiction. Now look at us. We've got a fuckin' empire: the publishing thing, the magazine, the porno DVDs—investments all over the fuckin' place. Not bad for a couple of fifty-year-old White boys from rural Nebraska, huh?"

Benton felt a bit uneasy about Ron's frequent expressions of racism, but he liked the money that was rolling in too much to complain too strongly about it.

"Bent, niggas call each other niggas these days," Ron had pointed out. "Why shouldn't we?"

"That's different," Benton explained. "Blacks have a right to call themselves whatever they want to call themselves."

"And so do I. This is America, thank God, and I have a right to say whatever I wanna say."

Benton smiled at his partner's absorption. The guy had a whole bunch of flaws, but he knew how to "make money off of niggas." Benton Marsh grimaced at the distasteful thought wandering through his mind.

"Ron, you busy?" he asked gently.

"Bent, take a look at this." Ron shoved the magnifying glass into his hand. Benton took the glass reluctantly.

"What am I looking at?" Benton asked. "What am I looking for?"

"Just take a long look at this broad's cunt lips."

Benton made a clinical study of the nude model's vaginal lips, as directed. It was . . . interesting, but any woman's cunt under a magnifying glass would be interesting, wouldn't it?

"It's a vagina, Ron. I can see that. Thanks to your careful instruction, I can now recognize the li'l beasties."

Sorry, Sarah, please forgive me, Benton thought to himself. *I'm talking to my money-making partner, Ron.*

Ron Wildstock took up another magnifying glass and wedged himself next to his partner.

"Bent, it's more than just a cunt. Look closely, and you'll see cum on this bitch's cunt. Start up at the top there and then travel slowly down south," Ron pointed out. "See that?! That's cum dripping from her clit. That's what gives her stuff that lipstick gloss look."

"I see it. So what's the big deal?"

His partner turned to stare at him with "that look," which he had grown to hate.

"Bent, don't you get it? This bitch has just had sex a few minutes before the shoot. Maybe the photographer put it to her or one of the guys on the set. In any case, it makes the whole thing a little more interesting, doesn't it?"

Benton nodded in agreement, suddenly feeling a little self-conscious, holding a magnifying glass in his hand as the photo section people swarmed around them.

"Uh, Ron, I wanted to get with you for a few minutes to talk about the new inventory. We have six new manuscripts in-house—"

"From the usual suspects—Icepick, Cummins, Mozel, Dawkins, Morrissey, and Hiker. Sounds like a fuckin' law firm, doesn't it?" Ron joked.

They exchanged smiles. Hollow Daze was always in court, being sued for one thing or another. Benton Marsh had laid out the guidelines for them. "What the hell, we go to court, pay them $25,000 and keep on raking in the gravy."

"So what's up, Bent?"

"I just wanted to get your opinion of Clay Block's critiques about the latest batch of manuscripts from our law firm."

"I read his critiques, and what is he saying?" Ron questioned. "We know what kind of shit these people write, and we know who's buying the shit—niggas."

Benton flinched involuntarily and glanced around to see if any of their Black staff was in the vicinity. Fortunately, there were only Whites. They were quite used to hearing their boss make racist comments. They pretended not to hear.

"So you approve?" Benton asked.

"Definitely. But I do have a couple of bones to pick. I'm beginning to get a bit pissed off with Dawkins. Seems that every time we publish one of his books, he starts bitchin' 'n' complainin' about the cover."

"Well, I guess he feels it's necessary. What the hell—let him bitch 'n' complain. We're making the money," Benton pointed out.

"Oh, one more thing, Bent . . . . I think we ought to cut Ruuth Morrissey loose."

"Why?"

"I'm getting sick and tired of her writing about how Black she is—she ain't," Ron explained.

"I know you're right, but her last book *Hood Thug* sold twelve thousand out of a fifteen thousand first printing."

"Leave her alone," Ron conceded. "The most important thing is the bottom line."

"Talk to you later. You wanna do lunch?"

"Can't. Got a whole bunch of naked bitches to look at for the next issue."

Ronald Cummins sat at his kitchen table, half high on heroin and cheap wine, casually studying the two roaches that were wandering from crumb to crumb. The lines on the legal pad in front of him seemed to ripple for a few moments. He reached up to take the ball-point from behind his right ear and held it over the legal pad for a few seconds, trying to think of what he wanted to write.

Daddy Smooth was done; it was at Hollow Daze House waiting for a cover and distribution. He nodded off for a few beats. Hollow Daze House—just as fucked up as I am. He came out of his nod, lit a cigarette, and nodded off again.

Maybe I'll write "Daddy Smooth's Revenge". Yeah, that's what I'll do, he thought. He took a strong pull on his cigarette and began to write, laboring over each word: Title: *Daddy Smooth's Revenge* by Ronald Cummins.

Revenge for what? From whom, by whom? Fuck it—from somebody on somebody. The lines on the legal pad seemed to straighten out a bit as he moved his pen with more fluency.

Daddy Smooth knew he had to get revenge on the thugs who had raped his momma; otherwise, they would just think of him as a punk bitch whom they could just run over if they wanted to.

Ronald stumbled up from the table and stutter-stepped over to the fridge to pull out a half bottle of rose wine. He sat back down, swallowing gulps of wine. He could feel his flow starting to happen. *If I can get through these first two or three pages, I'll be off into my latest masterpiece. Yeah,* Daddy Smooth's Revenge *is going to be fuckin' masterpiece. I can feel it in my bones.*

He nodded off briefly, but the nod was less profound. The heroin was loosening its grip, wearing off. *Think I better put* Revenge *on hold till after I've scored. It would be hell trying to write without a fix.* He started dressing to get out to his dealer's pad.

Jack Mozel screamed as he jacked himself up to a sitting position in bed. He stared at the television screen at the foot of the bed; an old John Wayne movie played. Sweat poured off of his body. He had labeled it the Iraq nightmare.

It seldom varied. He was the machine gunner on a Humvee rushing back to base camp in Baghdad after a three-day patrol. He was looking forward to a hot shower, a change of underwear, and a well-chilled, officially prohibited can of beer.

"As most of you men know, we're in a Muslim country. So out of respect, we won't be doing a lot of drinking—or should I say, no drinking at all?" Wink-wink. *Thanks, Sergeant Roughnuts.*

The IED that slammed into the vehicle decapitated the first lieutenant—the new guy who was always sticking his head out of the window. It blew all the people on the lower deck of the vehicle into huge chunks. He could close his eyes and visualize the chunks of flesh, the bulging eyes, and the blood everywhere.

They must've been using a stronger-than-usual explosive. That was the last conscious thought he had before he was air-evacuated to the base hospital. It was all a blur, even in his nightmare, except for the exploded bodies and the blood.

He went from the base hospital to the big hospital in Mannheim, Germany—real efficient shit, real efficient. It only took them three days to tell me that my dick and balls had been blown off and that I would be pissing like a li'l bitch for the rest of my life.

"Look, soldier, it could've been worse," a doctor had said. "We might be able to graft a new hose onto your body, but you can forget about having sex. Do you understand what I'm saying?"

What the hell was hard to understand about not having a dick and balls? With a cluster of shrapnel shards in your ass as a reminder.

Recovering in the hospital at Mannheim, he thought about committing suicide. Fortunately, they had a very hip brother from Bed-Stuy, New York—a big, rough-talking dude who resembled Chris Rock—doing the suicide counseling.

"Awright, Jack, let's lay this shit flat out on the table. The staff have caught you tryin' to bundle up pills 'n' shit, possibly to commit suicide. Okay?

"Awright, now here is the upside and the downside of the suicide thang," he'd said. "We've had a bunch of dudes come through here with suicide on their minds. We've saved a few and lost a few; the upside for those who have been successful at what they wanted to do is that they're gone; they've accomplished what they set out to do.

"But they've left emotional chaos behind them. Okay? I'm talking about wives, mothers, fathers, kids, cousins, a whole bunch of people that they basically fucked up when they decided to take their own lives.

"That's the thing about suicide; it has an unwholesome ripple effect. You're not just killing yourself; you're destroying other people as well—the ripple effect.

"So what happens if you contemplate suicide and you don't do it? Well, first off, your ass is still going to be alive, no matter what happens. That's the upside/plus factor. If you're alive, you may be able to work out a few things; if you're dead, it's all over."

"Well," I asked him, "What would you want to do if your dick and balls had been shot off, and your ass was half full of shrapnel?"

I have to give it to the brother; he didn't hesitate. "Well, I'm sure that I would think about suicide, under the circumstances, but I would pull back from that option. The reason why? Because life offers us many, many options, and death offers only one."

"Yeah, motherfucker, all that sounds cute, but how would you cope with what I got to deal with?"

"I don't know; I'm blind. What's suicide take on that?"

The brother's name was Gordon Bussey, and he helped me solve a whole bunch of problems. When I came out of the first phase of rehab, I knew that I was going to have to find a means of substitute gratification.

I had been fuckin' since I was in my teens, so I had a mental history to feed on. And I fed on it. In addition, I found myself drawn to the idea of writing about what was going on with me.

Writing became a sexual outsource for me. And lo 'n' behold, I discovered Hollow Daze. Or did they discover me? Well, *Death Time*, his latest, was on Benton Marsh's desk. It was time to start on something else.

CHAPTER 6

Aesthetics Anyone?

Harvey Dawkins strolled along the beach, pausing to watch the pelicans dive for fish and admire the grace and strength of the argumentative seagulls. He was feeling in a by-now-familiar low mood. It happened every time he turned a new book into Hollow Daze Publishing.

They're going to slap another one of those horrible-ass covers on the book; I just know they're going to do it, he thought. *I can hope for the best, but I have to expect the worse.*

"Benton, Ron, I've asked for this meeting with you guys to discuss the latest book cover."

"What's the problem, Harvey?"

"This is the problem. Look at this cover."

Ben Marsh and Ron Wildstock glanced at the trashy, lowercase tabloid photo on Dawkins's latest book and then exchanged smug looks. Ron Wildstock took the lead.

"Harvey, look," Ron began, "your books are selling pretty well, so what're you bitchin' about?"

"I'm bitchin' about this lousy-ass cover," Harvey complained. "The story is about a woman named Simone who falls in love with a younger man, discovers that he's gay, and what happens between them after that. It's a really sensitive story. The cover would mislead you into believing that this is some kind of video game, shoot-'em-up. It's not."

"So let me get this straight, Harvey. You're saying you don't like the cover?" Ron asked.

"That's exactly what I'm saying!"

"Well," Benton eased in suavely, "We're sorry you don't like the cover, but we're trying to appeal to our readers, not to our oversensitive authors."

"I am not being oversensitive."

He had to let it go at that. They weren't going to budge, he had better things to do, and it wouldn't serve any purpose to get angry and stay angry about a situation he couldn't control. Three of his best friends, would-be novelists and unpublished spoken-word artists, questioned his attachment to Hollow Daze Publishing House.—"Harvey, what are we missin' here? You say you hate these assholes at Hollow Daze, but you've just had your fourth book published by them. Why don't you go somewhere else?"

Harvey took a long, slow sip of his espresso, trying to think of the best answer to his friend's honest question.

"Jay, Frank, Kwame, you all are good brothers, good friends, but I have to tell you, you guys are not really tuned to what the reality is for the Black novelist—for *this* Black novelist."

"Maybe we're not; run it down for us."

Harvey picked up a flat rock and skip-bounced it off of the waves in front of him, flashing back to the coffee house conversation.

"It's true I'm not in love with Hollow Daze, and I would jump on the Random House wagon, the Little and Brown wagon, or any of the other majors, if they would accept me," he'd told his friends.

"I sent the four books that Hollow Daze published to about twenty-some-odd publishing houses. No go, nothing. One of the major Black publishing houses kept one of my novels for two years and then sent it back to me. They didn't even include a rejection notice. Ever heard of Third World Press?"

"Awe c'mon, man, you gotta be kiddin'."

"I kid you not; this is the real, buck-naked truth. I thought it was the subject matter that I was dealing with that was causing the problems. You know what I mean?

"I write about whatever I feel a passion about, and they don't want that kind of random writing. If you write a novel in one category, that's where you're supposed to stay for your whole creative life. If you start off with mystery, you gotta stay with mystery.

"Despite the bad covers, Hollow Daze doesn't do any editing—nothing. If they decide to publish your stuff, it doesn't matter what the subject matter is. I just turned in my fifth book to them the other day, and all of my books fit different genres: I have an urban fiction novel, a mystery novel, a romance novel, a historical novel, and the latest one is from a genre I invented. I'm calling it the Pan-African occult genre.

"I couldn't get away with that with any other publishing house that I can think of."

"So it doesn't sound like they're giving you such a bad time after all," Kwame noted.

"Kwame, it's about much more than that. It's a little like being cornered. I'm going to write, whether I get published or not. It's just in me to do this. You know the words in the song, 'fish gotta swim, birds gotta fly.' Well, I have to write. And I would definitely prefer being published by another publishing house, one that showed much more respect for its authors."

"So, okay, Benton Marsh, Ron Wildstock, Clay Block—the whole Hollow Daze Publishing crew is fucked up. So why deal with them?"

"Because I want to have my stuff published. I want people to know what's on my mind. I want to be famous, have lots of money, travel, and live the good life," Harvey explained.

"Gotta give it to you, bro. You're definitely determined to stick with it. What's your inspiration for this determination?"

"S-ola Salena," he answered without hesitation, "before we got married five years ago—"

"We were there, man, remember?"

"Well, before we got married, I was writing—no doubt about it—but I wasn't doing the kind of focused writing that you have to do in order for your stuff to become first rate."

He casually noticed Frank and Kwame lower their heads. *Well sorry, brothers, if the shoe happens to fit*, Harvey thought.

37

"S-ola does a lot of things with me, for me, that supply that little extra something that a lot of creative people need."

"Like what?"

"Well, like I can talk with her about what I'm doing and get some honest feedback. That's a little something extra, believe me. I wrote a book called, *The Memoirs of a Choirboy*, and she told me straight up, 'That's a lousy book.' You have to respect that kind of honesty.

"She encourages me to write. Don't tell me that you brothers haven't had some discouraging in your lives."

"You know we have, Harvey; you know we have."

"So I'm asking you to imagine the boost it would give you if you had somebody you loved, somebody who loved you, encourage you to do your thing. I'm sure all three of y'all have had somebody you wanted to be close to, but they didn't share your dream."

Jay, Frank, and Kwame nodded in agreement.

"S-ola empowers me. Do you understand what I'm saying? Right now she's the one who supplies the balance about this Hollow Daze thing. If I weren't being published by Hollow Daze, I wouldn't have anything out there, and I would be twice as frustrated.

"She's telling me, 'Don't bog yourself down with negative thoughts about Hollow Daze, Benton, that crap. Just keep on writing as well as you can, and you'll be able to write your way out of their bag.' She's a dreamer with a firm grip on reality, and that's good for me, for our relationship."

"Yeah, you got lucky, H.D."

"S-ola got any sisters?"

"Yeah, but they're all down in Texas, and they're not like her."

Harvey jammed his hands down in his pockets and strolled back to his car. It was time to get back to the drawing board. *Time Out* was finished, turned into the belly of the beast. It was time to do the proposal that his Muslim friend, Waheed Ali, had asked him to do three months ago.

And he was looking forward to seeing S-ola; he hadn't seen her for three whole hours.

Ruuth Morrissey lay in bed on her side, glaring at the broad. Black back of her latest lover. How would a Black woman handle the situation? What would a Black woman say to her man after he had trotted home at two o'clock in the morning three nights in row, reeking with the smell of cheap perfume on his body. And what about the lipstick smudges on the right shoulder of his blue shirt?

She laced her hands behind her cornrowed head, thinking.

Maybe I should talk to him about this in the morning. What would I talk to him about? About seeing another woman? Shit, he was "seeing" two other women when I met him.

She did a mental review of the last six men she had been intimate with over the course of the past six years. They had all been African-Americans, Blacks, and they had all been unfaithful to her. Why? That was the question she wanted an answer to.

I'm five six; I'm stacked; I have a beautiful ass; I'm smart, with two masters from a couple prestigious schools; I have rich parents who are willing to bail me out of any bad financial situation; I'm a published author, courtesy of Hollow Daze Publishing House; and I keep hooking up with guys who basically treat me like trash, Ruuth thought to herself.

"Hey, lookahere, Ruuuuth, you ain't my fuckin' Momma, and you sho' ain't my Daddy, so what the fuck is up with you about this being-on-time bullshit?!"

"Well, I told you I was preparing veal scallopinis, and we were going to have tiramizu for dessert, and—"

"Hey, what the fuck do I care about some veal scaloppini or tiramisu? I ain't into all that foreign food bullshit. I stopped off with some of my homies to have a couple of fish tacos. Okay? You know what I'm sayin'?"

Well, so much for Melvin Collins.

"Hey Ru-uth, why you be callin' me on my cell all the time? It's like you yankin' my chain or somethin'."

"I was just concerned about you, Jerry. That's all. I wasn't trying to yank your chain, as you call it." Bye-bye Jerry.

"Look, Ruuth baby, I need twenty-five hundred dollars to do this thang I'm tryin' to do."

"Fred, I already loaned you two thousand for your other thang. When are you gonna repay me?"

"Hey, what the fuck you talkin' about?! You *gave* me two thousand. You didn't loan me shit."

"Well, what about this twenty-five hundred? Is that supposed to be a gift or a loan?"

"It all depends on you, Ruuthie baby. Is it a gift or a loan? You know I need it, or else I wouldn't be askin'. C'mere, baby Ruuth, gimme some sugar. You my woman—you know what I'm sayin'?"

You know what I'm sayin'? Two grand for one thang, twenty-five hundred bucks for another thang. Ciao, Fred baby.

Firefly, the rapper.

"Fire, you know I had some serious doubts about us being able to get together."

"Why you say that?"

"Well, basically because I'm older than you. I'm going on thirty, and you're only nineteen."

"That ain't no real big thang. I done fucked ol' bitches before. You know what I'm sayin'?"

Old bitch at thirty? The Fire went out, taking eight thousand dollars' worth of her jewelry with him.

Enter the Dragon—Bad Boy Brown—for a few furious moments in bed.

"Bad Boy, look . . . we've been in bed for two weeks now."

"So what? We got a fridge fulla food, a bar fulla booze, some good herb to smoke, you done paid all our bills 'n' shit. What else do we need to do?"

"I need to write."

"Fuck writin'. That's like doin' your homework all the time."

Bye-bye, Bad Boy Brown.

And now Jun Jun. She turned to stare at his broad, black back again. No sense trying to think of anything diplomatic to say to him about his infidelities and his lack of morality and self-control.

"Hey, Ru-uth, what's up with you, girl? You ain't my momma. You know what I'm sayin'?"

She didn't really want to get out of bed, but she rationalized herself into doing it. What the hell, if I'm going to lay here half the night thinking about how miserable I am, how fucked up this shit is, then I may as well get started on the outline for my next novel for Hollow Daze House—*I Was White, He Was Black.*

The writing life has many layers, flavors . . .

Alice W. Hiker took careful notice of the trio of well-dressed, African American women approaching her table. They looked thirty-ish, slightly overweight, well manicured and pedicured, successful. And they were clutching copies of her latest Hollow DazePublishing House release—*Open Sesame*, "a very sexy novel by a Black woman, for Black women."

She was attending another book signing, this one at the Eso Won Book store in Leimert Park. After four books published by Hollow Daze House but completely *un*promoted by them, she knew what to do. *I'm gonna get out here and peddle this bad boy*, she said to herself.

She crisscrossed the city of Los Angeles and the areas nearby, bugging bookstore owners and managers to bring *Open Sesame* into their stores. She was persistent, positive, and upbeat. And it was paying off, in dribbles—slowly but surely. The Eso Won signing was a good example. She had talked to James Fugate, one of the stores owners, six different times before he finally agreed to have her do a book signing.

"The first Saturday in August," he finally agreed. "That okay for you, Alice?"

"That'll be just fine, James, just fine."

She had been sitting at her table for four hours already; one book sold to a freckle-faced old White man who had read a couple of paragraphs about her new book in the *Watts News* biweekly newspaper.

"The minute I read about your appearance, I knew I had to come."

"Well, thank you for coming, Mr . . . . ?"

"Thorvald Pedersen," he answered. "Most of my friends call me Thor."

"Well, thanks again for coming, Mr. Thor. Hope you enjoy *Open Sesame*."

"I'm sure I will," he assured her as he shuffled out of the store.

One sale in four hours. She felt like standing up to do a big tent-circus-barker-pitch.

"Step right this way, folks! Come take a look at the two-headed writer! It's all right-here-in-here-in-her latest! *Open Sesame*—buy one, get one free! Step right up, folks!"

The trio of African American women arranged themselves in front of her table. They were a beautiful spectrum—one chocolate, one beige, and one light beige. Alice W. Hiker put on her public relations face; one could never tell—they might be Hollywood producers.

"Good to see you, sisters. I see you have the book of the day!"

The trio loosened up immediately. Miss Chocolate spoke for them. "Sister Alice, you are too much. *Open Sesame* is a mindblower! You hear me? A mindblower!"

Alice was prepared to deal with rejection, maybe casual acceptance, but not a wholesale embrace.

"Look, I'm going to spend another fifteen minutes here, and then I'll be free. Would you sisters like to go around the corner for a drink?" Alice asked.

"We'd love to," Miss Not-too-Beige responded. "And you'll autograph our books?"

"With pleasure."

CHAPTER 7

Runnin It Down

The Blues Room at two o'clock in the afternoon was a far shot from being what it was at two o'clock in the morning—a small stage in the east corner, a medium-sized dance floor in front of the stage, Formica-coated tables for four daisy-chained around the dance floor.

Alice and her three fans pulled up chairs and occupied a table in the center of the room. A few pouchy-eyed ol' timers nursing beer bottles at the bar on the west side of the room gave their hips and breasts look of lustful approval. The beer-barrel shaped bartender gave them a minute to settle in place before he wedged himself from behind the bar.

"What can I get you ladies?"

Alice W. Hiker, a frequent visitor to the Blues Room, knew the bartender's limitations. She had made the mistake of ordering a daiquiri twice and a gin and tonic twice, each one more disastrous than the last. The nighttime waitress pulled her coat.

"Uh, honey, Bob is good at pouring drinks and opening beer bottles, but he ain't good at making drinks."

From that point on, she played it safe.

"I'll have a shot of Jack and a Bud," Alice said.

Her fan base of three exchanged looks with each other and with her; that was reaffirmation enough.

"Uh, we'll have the same."

Alice gave them the low down as Bob waddled back behind the bar to pour four generous shots of Jack Daniels and to find four of the coldest Buds in his fridge for these lovely ladies.

"Uh, Bob is good at pouring drinks and opening beer bottles, but he ain't good at making drinks," she whispered.

"Oh God, I'm glad you told us. There's absolutely nothing I hate worse than a badly made Margarita."

"Or a Daiquiri."

"Or a Manhattan."

It only took two or three sips of Jack and a couple of swallows of beer for the atmosphere to warm up.

"Alice . . . can we call you Alice?" one of the women asked.

"Sure, by all means," Alice replied. "And you are?"

The three women introduced themselves in succession.

"I'm Gloria."

"I'm Bernice."

"I'm Coretta."

"Pleased to meet you," Alice said with a nod. "Now then, you wanted your books autographed?"

"I definitely want my book signed, but I also wanna ask some questions." Gloria's sharply honed English was already beginning to blur around the edges a bit.

"Shoot!"

"My first question is, what made you decide to write a sex manual?"

"Is that what you think it is?"

"Well, I can't say for sure if it is or not, but you certainly got pretty graphic in here about what men and women should do with each other sexually."

"Like right here, in chapter two, third paragraph, where you wrote, 'Maurice loved to play *open sesame* with me. This was a game he had invented where he would knock his big ol' black dick against the outer petals of my vagina, and I would let him in to enjoy all of the treasures inside.'"

Bob the bartender glanced over at their table and exchanged knowing looks with his regulars. These were obviously "innerlectuals" from the bookstore around the corner. What else could they be? Each of them with a book in her hands.

"How about chapter six? 'I really enjoyed watching Nick's eyes rollback up in his head when I gently nibbled on his knob. Poor Nick had no tolerance whatsoever when I tongue-whipped his jones.'"

"Chapter eight, second paragraph, y'all. 'When Mike shot his wad in me, I always had the sensation of having a space rocket explode inside of me. I've never felt an ejaculation that strong. I think Mike must've had jet fuel in his balls.'"

Alice signaled to the bartender for another round; her guests were beginning to enjoy themselves.

"Alice, girl, I just have to ask you. Is this autobiographical?" Coretta asked bluntly.

Alice Hiker smiled. It wasn't the first time she had been asked that question. "Coretta, let me put it to you this way. It would be impossible, I think, for any honest writer to write anything unless there was a bit of autobiographical stuff in there."

"So this is you? Your experiences?"

"I didn't say that. I'm saying that I don't leave *me* behind when I write."

Bob the bartender circled their table, pouring the leftover dribs of Jack Daniels into the new shot glasses. His expert eyes told him that they weren't "serious" drinkers, and one or two of them were going to be pie-eyed by the time they were ready to go.

"Alice, no matter if it's autobiographical or not, the thing that impressed me the most was your honesty. When you write about nibbling on Nick's knob, for example. I'm trying to write myself, but I would never be able to write about nibbling on any man's knob."

"Why not? You mean to tell me that you've never nibbled on your lover's knob?" Alice questioned.

She could tell from the way the three women ringed around the table took agitated, simultaneous sips of their Jack that she had touched a nerve. Gloria cleared the whiskey from her palate with a gulp of beer.

"Well, speaking for myself only, let me say this. I've only been intimate with four men in my whole life. One of them was my ex-husband, and we never went there. I mean, me, I never thought about doing anything like that!"

"Why not?" Alice the writer probed.

"It just never came up."

The women released a group laughing fit that startled the regulars. *Uh-oh, they gettin' drunk over there*, Bob thought, smiling in their direction. *Jack and beer, huh? Let's see how this plays out.*

"Ha-ha, ha-ha, uh, Gloria, I can understand what you're saying, but there are times we have to bring it up. You know what I mean?"

Gloria, Bernice, and Coretta were exactly the audience she was trying to reach with *Open Sesame*. They were still young, attractive, and well educated but were sexually repressed.

"Alice, I can appreciate what you're saying, but you know how hard it is, sometimes, to get away from that puritanical thing our mothers put on us—keep your dress down and your panties up."

They shred a laugh about that one too. Alice felt like the moderator on a sex info panel or a slightly salacious guide.

"I remember that too. Let me ask you this. Which one of you sisters is married, or are you all married?"

"You're looking at the Divorcee's Club. All of us have been married. I've been married twice."

"I don't want to get personal or anything, but would you agree that an *anemic* sex life, a malnourished sex life might have had something to do with your divorces?"

Bernice pursed her lips thoughtfully. Gloria took a long sip of her Jack, and Coretta nodded seriously.

"Yeah, yeah. To be honest, I think we'd all have to say yes." Coretta spoke up. "Gloria, you agree?—Bernice?"

"I don't want to suggest that a robust sex life is the solution, the key to matrimonial bliss, because a whole lot of other factors play a part too, but it is important. It was one of the strongest reasons for me to write *Open Sesame.*

"I've talked to so many sisters, just like we're talking now, and I have to admit I was a bit surprised to discover how repressed so many of us are. We wear beautiful, sexy clothes; we work out and have beautiful bodies. But we find it very hard to get up off a good piece of pussy."

She wished for a camera to record the expressions on their intelligent faces. They suddenly looked dumb, fearful.

"Alice, you know what I'm gonna ask you?" Gloria spoke up. "What is a good piece . . . ?"

"Gloria, I can't answer that,—there are too many variables. I think a lot of it depends on the man. Some men may think that this is a good piece; another man may think that's a good piece. I have a theory that pussy is like a delicious stew—it's only as good as the spices and the spoon you use to stir it with."

They cracked up again. Alice signaled for another round.

"Alice, we know you have to go; otherwise, we would hold onto you for another three hours. But I just have to ask this last question. Why Hollow Daze Publishing House?"

"I'm tempted to say, why not Hollow Daze? But I know what you mean. You're referring to the gruesome cover on *Open Sesame.*"

"And the other ones too. Ugh!"

Alice laughed with them, a bittersweet laugh.—"Ha-ha . . . let me be completely honest with you. I would definitely have preferred Random House, Little and Brown, Dutton, one of the majors, or even Third World Press or one of the other African-American publishing houses. But you know what they said to me?—Thanks, but no thanks."

"Thanks, but no thanks, that's what they told me."

"But why, girlfriend?" Gloria pressed. "You're an excellent writer, the subject matter is compelling, and you definitely have a fan base. I'm in marketing. I know what I'm talking about."

"Gloria, I know you know what you're talking about, but what you're talking about has to do with what might be called 'normal markets.' The place where the African-American writer, male or female, *falls* is an abnormal place."

Alice studied the blank expressions on their faces for a pregnant moment before plunging into the subject.

"Look, it would take at least two semesters going to class three days a week to take you into what America does with the African-American writer. Don't misunderstand me. This place fucks with its intellectuals—period—but there is a special shelf reserved for the African-American writer, so-called intellectual.

"Let's go back to why I wound up with Hollow Daze House. I was really counting on the Black publishing houses to publish me, because I thought they had access to my core consumer base."

"Us," Coretta announced.

"Yes, Black females in America. But the brothers who control whatever they control in the publishing business rejected me too."

"But why?" Bernice asked.

"It definitely had to do with sex. First off, as I'm sure you three know, most middle-class African-Americans tend to be quite puritanical." Alice paused to give them a chance to agree or disagree with her. They nodded in agreement.

"The myth of the oversexed Black has been seriously overdone. Now then, having said that, please remember that most of the members of the Black publishing establishment, such as it is, are college-educated, middle-class guys. They may not have started out that way, but that's the way they became. I hate to equate being middle class with being puritanical, but it just seems to work out that way. I think it's hypocritical puritanism, but it's still prude stuff, no matter how you slice it."

The bartender was at their table with a fresh round the minute Alice raised her hand.

"So you're saying they wouldn't publish your work because it's sexy?" Bernice asked.

"Bernice, if you weren't a woman, I would kiss you."

They got a big kick out of that one, laughing loudly and high-fiving each other around the table.

"That's it in a nutshell. I actually had an interview with a well-known Black publisher in Chicago who told me, straight up, 'Alice, there's no need for you to be writing this kind of filth. I think you're just trying to shock us, to be naughty for the sake of being naughty.'"

"Nawww, you got to be kiddin'!" Coretta gasped.

"Coretta, cross my heart 'n' hope to die! That's what the brother said. I don't want to take you into the written rejection slips. One of them said, 'We do not publish pornography.'"

"*Open Sesame* is not porno," Gloria declared and took a long sip of her Jack. *Shit!*

"I agree with you. I didn't think it was then, and I don't think it is now, but the reason I'm running all of this down to you is to explain how I wound up at Hollow Daze House."

One of the regulars put money into the old-fashioned Art Deco juke box standing in the northeast corner of the Blues Room, and a song off an ancient Muddy Water's record began to play. "Ah'm uhh *mayne*, spelled m . . . a . . . n!" The music seemed to offer Alice W. Hiker a perfect accompaniment for her story.

"After being rejected by just about everybody—some of the White rejections bordered on sheer racism, 'We do not publish ethnic material'—I finally decided to go to Hollow Daze House. It wasn't an easy decision to make, because I had seen their book covers."

"Ugh!"

"Double ugh!"

"And I knew that they had a reputation for being somewhat raunchy, but I felt it was necessary to take a chance with them. What you have to remember is this—if your works are not exposed, if they're not in the public eye, then you remain anonymous. Gloria, you're into marketing, am I right?"

"Yeah, you're right about that. You gotta show what you got if you want to sell it. Nobody wants to buy a pig in the poke."

"Damn, Gloria, there ya go again, talkin' all that down, down stuff. What's a pig in the poke mean?"

"Them who knows does not tell, and them who tells does not know," Gloria joked.

Alice Hiker made a quick study of the women around the table. They were at stage one of being semidrunk. She recognized the groove, because she was halfway there herself.

"Go 'head on, Alice, don't pay them no mind."

"Well, what can I say? I submitted my first manuscript to Hollow Daze."

"Was that *Lickin 'n' Stickin*?"

"No, that was the second one. *Love Them Hips* was my first one, and then the third was *The Quiet Vagina*, the fourth was *Momma's Baby, Daddy's Maybe*. And now *Open Sesame*."

"I've read all of 'em 'cept *The Quiet Pussy*," Gloria slurred.

"It's *Quiet Vagina*," Gloria, *Quiet Vagina*," Bernice reminded her.

"What's the difference?" Gloria threw the question out, shaking her well-permed head in time to the Muddy Waters classic—"I say *mmmm . . . ayne!*"

"The difference, girlfriend, is that vaginas are quiet, and pussies are loud," Bernice noted. "Ain't that right, Alice?"

The table was bubbling with good vibes, animated by the spicy subject matter, the blues music, and the Jack Daniels.

"Bernice, I can't claim to be an authority on either one. I haven't had that much experience."

Her flip answer triggered contagious laughter. A few other people had filtered into the Blues Room and looked at the quartet of hard-drinkin' women with real affection. They may look a li'l booshie but they're knockin' back them Jacks 'n' a beer, so they must be cool.

Coretta held up her well-manicured hands for quiet. "Will y'all please chill? Let Alice finish what she was sayin'. Go 'head, Alice."

The Muddy Waters classic was followed by a less robust tune, B. B. King's "The Thrill is Gone." Gloria got a bit misty eyed.

"Well, there's not much else to say. Hollow Daze decided to take a chance on me, and you're holding the results in your hands," Alice said. "I could add that Benton Marsh; his partner, Ron Wildstock; and the editor, Clay Block, are not fun people to deal with.

"Benton wants to make jokes all the time, like he's trying to entertain a small child. Ron Wildstock may or may not be a member of the Aryan nation, and Block is a heavy drinking gay guy. I give him credit for being the most sensitive of the trio, but that doesn't mean a whole lot.

"I suspect they cook the books. There is a stipulation in their contracts that say you have to give them a month's notice if you wanted to have an accountant go through their books. I don't think it would matter in any case. They would have more than enough time to switch the books."

"Motherfuckers!"

The rest of the group were startled by Coretta's loudly expressed profanity.

"Oh yeah, Coretta, you got that right—they're motherfuckers, but they got the only game in town. They don't promote their books very much, which is why I was at Eso Won today. But I have to say once again, either you're in the public eye or you're anonymous.

And if you're anonymous, no one will buy your books. It's kind of a catch-22."

"Oh yes, it's about all of that and much more. A lot of people are not hip to the business of publishing. They think you give a manuscript to a publisher, he publishes it, it becomes a best seller, and everybody lives happily ever after. There's a helluva lot more to it than that."

"Holly Daze House—don't they publish that gruesome little *Playboy* knock off? *Playboy* in Black, I heard somebody call it."

"You're talking about *Duh Playa*. That's Ron Wildstock's baby," Alice explained. "He seems to get his jollies from pictures of crackhead, nude Black prostitutes in garter belts."

"Garter belts? Those are from the eighteenth century or something, aren't they?"

"Probably. It doesn't matter with him. As one of the sisters who works at Hollow Daze explained to me, 'they were looking for a way to lose enough money to get a tax write off or something.' She didn't understand it, and I don't understand it either, but it seems to be working for them.

"In addition to the magazine, you know they do porno movies and a whole bunch of other stuff."

Bob the bartender waddled over to their table with a fresh round of drinks.

"Oh, we didn't order another round."

"This is compliments of the gentleman at the end of the bar—the one with the egg-yolk-yellow suit on and the white silk tie."

They weren't squares, and they had all had enough experience to recognize a "playa" when they saw one.

The yellow-suited man would follow up his "complimentary drinks" with a visit to their table for a flowery little chat and then try to single one of them out for "further exploration."

"What is our friend drinking?" Alice asked the bartender.

"Uh, he's into that Hennessey."

"Well, thank him for us and give him four cognacs, with our compliments."

The bartender, hip to all games played in the Blues Room, smiled broadly at the exchange. He hurried to pour the playa four snifters of cognac. The playa looked startled for a moment and then turned to take a sip from each snifter as he lifted each glass in a silent toast to them. *Slick-ass bitches*, he thought.

"Well, sisters, looks like it's about that time—salud!"

They clinked their shot glasses together and poured the Jack down the hatch. Gloria decided to cover the check with her gold-standard credit card. "This is on me," she noted.

The four women staggered up from their seats, feeling the full effects of an afternoon of whisky sippin' and beer drinkin'. They made a grand exit, doing a little rumba movement as they passed the yellow-suited playa man.

"Y'all goin'?" he questioned. "It ain't even started happenin' yet."

"Yeah," Coretta sang out above the music and the developing crowd. "We gotta go. We got jobs to go to tomorrow."

The playa curled his lips down with contempt. *Jive-ass bitches.*

Outside of the Blues Room, the warm air of an August evening in Los Angeles sobered them up a pinch. What now? "Hey, Alice, you didn't sign our books."

"See what that bad whisky will do to you?" She took out her ball-point and signed each one in succession: "I lit my fire, I greased my skillet, and I cooked. Alice W. Hiker."

"That was fun; we have to do it again—soon."

"Yeah, I think it would be fun just to see what Mr. Yellow Suit is all about."

"Forget it, Gloria, he's a potential fire hazard, and you don't want to play with that."

"I heard that."

"Here, why don't you take our cards so that we can stay in touch?"

"Oh, incidentally, Alice, I'm having a little gathering at my place this weekend. Think you might be able to come?"

"And bring some books. We'll set up a li'l place for you if that's cool with you?"

"I'm looking forward to it already. Where are you sisters parked?"

"We didn't drive. We thought it would be good exercise to walk down here."

"We live just up the hill here, off of Vernon."

"Great. See you this weekend. What day?"

"Saturday."

They exchanged last hugs and waved tipsy good-byes. Alice watched them weave up the street, laughing and joking about their afternoon in the Blues Room. She watched them hustle across Crenshaw before she made her decision. Think I'll go back in here for a night cap to see what this yellow suit is talking about. He might be the subject matter for a new book, *The Man in the Yellow Suit.*

CHAPTER 8

To Be Or Not?

Clay Block sprawled back in his adjustable chair, alternatively sucking on a well-rolled joint and sipping from a glass of De War's scotch, staring at a silent television screen.

This fuckin' place is so dull without Paul. The thought was like a sharp pain. *Paul is gone. Paul is gone.* He lit the joint, took a deep hit, placed the smoking joint in an ash tray on his right side, and took a sip of scotch.

"Clay, what the fuck is the matter with you?! Are you gonna continue to waste your creative powers down there at that dreadful li'l Hollow Daze Publishing House? Look at what they're doing, what they're about. They're into exploiting simple, naïve Black writers, and you've become a part of the machinery."

"*Paul, don't be cruel, it's a way to earn a living and pay our bills.*"

"I don't care to have my bills paid for by slave labor, thank you."

Paul is gone. Maybe he'll be back after he discovers that there is no one out there who loves him as much as I do. Clay stumbled out of his chair to go to the fridge for more ice for his scotch. He paused to look at himself in the mirror flanking the corridor to the kitchen.

Look at you. You're a fucking mess—no wonder your man left you, Clay thought. *No, that's not true; he didn't leave me because my hair hasn't been combed or because my clothes are wrinkled or because I've lost thirty pounds in the past two months. He's gone because of some fucked up sense of ethics.*

Clay emptied ice cubes out of a tray, dropped three of them into his glass, and staggered back to his chair in the front room to drink more scotch and smoke more dope.

Why should I put my ass on the line by telling these people to read between the lines in the contracts? What purpose would it serve to tell them that their contracts bind them to Hollow Daze for much too long? Should I tell them that they're not being given a truthful accounting of their royalties? Why should I get involved with their lives?

Icepick Slim, *Pimpin'*, a bunch of immoral trash.

"Skip the morality factor, Clay. Do you think this shit will sell?" Benton's words echoed in his head.

"I'm sure a certain class of people will buy it."

"That's all I wanted to hear."

Ronald Cummins, *Daddy Smooth*, sensational nonsense, no redeeming social values at all—violence for the sake of violence.

Jack Mozel, *Death Time*. Jack is a nice guy, but how long can you relive Iraq? I guess that's what post-traumatic stress disorder will do to you.

Dawkins, *Time Out*. The best of the six, the best period. Why doesn't he break away from Hollow Daze? Well, who the hell am I to talk?

He fumbled for the remote, channel surfed for a minute, and stopped at the all-news station. President Obama was giving another one of his sensible, down-to-earth speeches. It was such a relief to finally have a president who could actually speak an unmangled brand of English. *Good-bye, Bush, you did enough damage.*

Clay turned the sound up for a few seconds to listen to Obama's mellow baritone and then tuned the sound off again. I don't want to hear anybody speak; I don't want to try to figure anything out. He took a slug of Scotch and fired up the joint again.

Ruuth Morrissey. The bio of Zora Neal Hurston wasn't bad, but why does she insist on trying to write everything from a *Black* perspective? A walking identity crisis, that woman.

Alice W. Hiker, *Open Sesame*. A beautiful writer with a strong sense of satire, too damned good for the Benton Marsh/Ron Wildstock plantation.

Obama flashed his big smile at him. Well, it seemed to be at him. He was drunk from the scotch and high from the marijuana, a yo-yo state he enjoyed unless it caused him to vomit.

Ten years ago, when I was forty, what would've happened if I had stood up to Benton Marsh? Clay wondered. *I would've been fired. Or else I would've been given more respect. Well, what the hell, no matter what you said, Paul, you can't have everything.*

He tilted himself back in his adjustable chair and stared at the ceiling. *Maybe I'll finish that novel I started ten years ago. No, what sense would that make? We have more than enough half-baked novelists in the world already.*

Maybe I'll revise the White Mountain Apache book. He smiled up at the ceiling. *Imagine, me, a drunk-ass, failed novelist, the editor for a blaxploitation publishing house, a gay man without a man, a fool for dope, an expert on the religious practices of the White Mountain Apache Native Americans, an anthropological binge I've been on for thirty years.*

Why the White Mountain Apache People? One of the elders had told him, "Don't worry. This is what you are supposed to be doing." So every summer for the past thirty years, he had spent with the White Mountain Apaches in Arizona—or what was left of them.

"Cl'aay, don't worry of us, we were here when the nonpeople arrived, and we will be here after they have gone," the elder had told him. "Our religion tells us of this."

Clay fired up the joint again. Hollow Daze House Publishing Company flashed across his brain like a huge neon sign. He blinked his eyes, trying to blot the horrible, garish lighting from tripping him out. No good. He felt trapped by the neon lights.

I'm fifty fuckin' years old. Jesus H. Christ! He leaned forward in his chair and started crying. He couldn't really identify the reason for his tears, but they were there. The tears stopped as suddenly as they had started.

The harsh neon lights softened, but the flickering lights still spelled out "Hollow Daze House Publishing Company." He leaned back in his chair to stare up at the ceiling.

Where else can I go, at fifty years old, to stay drunk all day? The thought stayed on his brain as he passed over into a familiar booze-weed space.

<u>Conflicts:</u>

Benton Marsh and Ron Wildstock against the writers. It's months after their books have been published, and they're all dissatisfied by one thing or the other.

Icepick Slim (suavely)

"Benton, I cannot, for the life of me, understand why you must continue to resist my efforts to receive an honest accounting of my royalties. Every where I look people are reading my book *Pimpin'*, and you're telling me that sales have been poor?"

Benton Marsh (slightly pissed)

"Look, Icepick, royalties are not determined by how many people read the book but by how many copies of the book are sold."

Icepick Slim (puzzled)

"Would you be kind enough to run that past me again?"

Benton

"It's simple. All of the people you think you're seeing with copies of your book may not have bought those books."

Icepick (steaming up)

"So what're you saying, Benton, is I'm being delusional?"

Benton

"No, no, no! Pick, I'm not even suggesting anything like that. I think you're a brilliant cat . . . uh, dude . . . uh, guy, but I think you're giving us a bit of a rough patch on this one."

Icepick (coldly)

"So what does that mean?"

Benton

"It means that I think you're not being fair about this; you're not willing to listen to the Hollow Daze House's side of the story."

Icepick

"Benton, I've listened to the Hollow Daze House side of the story, and frankly speaking, it smells a bit foul. I'd like to have my accountant come up in here and check your books."

Benton

"Uh, Pick—"

Icepick Slim

"The name is *Icepick*, Benton. Don't forget that."

Benton (false bravado)

"Okay, awready. It sounds like you're threatening me."

Icepick Slim

"No, no, Benton, I'm not threatening you. I think, if you do a li'l research about me, you'll find that I never make threats. Consult some of my ex-hos if you like. And the proper pronunciation of my name is Icepick Slim. Get it, Benton? My name is Icepick Slim."

Benton (feeling threatened)

"Okay, okay, Icepick Slim. What I'm saying to you, in reply to your request about your accountant and all that, is that we would be perfectly happy to accommodate you. However, if you would really like to have your own accountant rip into us, I think you should go to paragraph 42b/section k, about the acceptance of 'foreign accountants.'"

Icepick

"Foreign accountants? What's the deal here? You think I'm bringing in people from Spain or Iceland or wherever?"

Benton

"Uh, no. 'Foreign accountants' means accountants who are not the Hollow Daze House payroll."

Icepick

"So my foreign accountants would be unacceptable because they're not Hollow Daze House accountants—people who are paid by Hollow Daze House?"

Benton

"Awe, Icepick, why do you want to get yourself all wrapped up in stuff like this? You're a writer—an artist."

Icepick Slim

"Benton, you seem to want to forget that I was a pimp. That's the clothesline that capitalism is hung up on, dig it?"

Benton

"Huh? What's that mean?"

"Ronald Cummings! Good to see you, big guy!"

"Fuck you talkin' about, Benton?! You ain't glad to see me. Why you be talkin' all this kinda bullshit to me? You oughta check yo'self, Benton—yo' slip is showin'."

"Awright, Ronald Cummings, let's say I'm *not* glad to see you," Benton retorted. "How's that?"

"Well, it sounds a helluva lot more honest."

"Great. So I'm *not* glad to see you. Now, that we've got that part squared away. You asked for an appointment. What can I do for you?"

"I want an advance," Ronald said.

"We already gave you an advance."

"That was for my last book. I'm talkin' 'bout an advance for my next book."

"Sorry, Ronald, we can't do that," Benton replied.

"Why the fuck not?!"

"Well, uh, because . . . uhh . . . it's too risky," Benton explained, fumbling over his words.

"What the fuck does that mean, Ben-ton?"

"That means just what I said. 'Spose we give you an advance for your next book, and somethin' happens to you."

"Awe c'mon, Benton, you know ain't nothin' gon' happen to me."

"You're still doing that drug thing, right?" Benton asked.

"What the fuck's that got to do with anything?" Ronald snapped back.

"Well, maybe nothing, maybe a lot. In any case, we don't do advances for books that we haven't received, that we don't have in-house."

"You, Ron Wildstock, Clay Block—all of y'all is a bunch o' chickenshit motherfuckers. You know that?"

"I've been called worse. Now, if our meeting is over, I'd like to get back to work," Benton said. "I have a lot of stuff to do, contracts to deal with."

"So if I bring in a manuscript, you'll give me an advance, huh?"

"It depends on whether Clay accepts it," Benton explained.

"Awe kiss my ass, Benton. You the motherfucker who makes the decisions around here," Ronald said. "If you say yes, it goes. If you say no, it doesn't go."

"Ronald Cummings, I don't have the time or the inclination to debate with you about this."

"Y'all is just a bunch of chickenshit motherfuckers. You know that?"

"You already told me that, remember?"

The dream was threatening to become a nightmare again. Jack Mozel made himself remember that all he had to do was force his eyelids open, and the nightmare would have nowhere to go, no ground to breed on. He had to push hard and grunt a bit to force his eyelids open.

Eyes wide open now, he stared up at the fan whirling slowly in the ceiling. *There was a fan in the ceiling of the house we broke into, in Fallujah, but it wasn't working,* he thought. *There was nothing moving in that house when we busted in at two o'clock in the morning.*

Who fired first? Who screamed? "Look out he's armed!" Who was responsible for a family of fifteen being shot to pieces?

"Collateral damage, justified reaction to the situation." That's what the report noted. The rest of the language in the official report/review of the action simply served to prevent anybody from being accused of murder. The official report/review was signed sealed and filed: "no case."

We killed those people. We murdered a whole family. They didn't have any weapons. They woke up in the middle of the night to find a bunch of uniformed men wearing night goggles rampaging through their house. They jumped up, and we started shooting—men, women, and children. The oldest was a woman eighty-eight years old, and the youngest was a three-month-old baby.

"Collateral damage, justified reaction to the situation."

Jack believed it was deeper than that; it was a revenge thing, retaliation for the killing of four of their guys the day before. Coming back from a long patrol, they'd been hit by an "improvised roadside device"—a fuckin' bomb that tore four guys to shreds. *That's why we murdered that innocent family,* Jack thought.

What Jack couldn't figure out was why they had killed the two teenage boys they'd caught on the streets after curfew?

"Waste the little raghead bastards, it'll keep us from fightin' 'em later on." That had been Sergeant Maxwell's "suggestion."

61

How many others did we kill? Jack wondered. *How much "collateral damage" did we do?*

Jack reached over to his night table for his cigarettes and glanced at the clock nearby. 2:15 a.m. It was always 2:15 a.m. *So what the fuck is gonna happen to me? Am I 'sposed to have a nightmare at two fifteen in the morning for the rest of my life?*

He propped himself up in bed, lit his cigarette, and took a deep hit. He decided he needed a drink. He climbed out of bed and padded through his apartment to the kitchen—to the half-empty bottle of Jack Daniels on the sideboard. He poured himself a half water glass of the liquor and took a long drink.

The pungent bourbon smell and the raw flavor made him grimace. *Ah yeah . . . that's it, that's what I need.* He leaned against the kitchen sink and stared out of the window at a full moon.

Drunk again. After two tours of duty in Iraq, slightly wounded by shrapnel in the back of his head, back, and buttocks but terribly wounded by his experiences, he had returned from the war. Drunk again.

He filled the water glass with Jack and lurched through his apartment to the dining room table where he did his writing. *So Ron Wildstock and Benton Marsh want me to become the editor of that little fucked up piece of crap they call Duh Playa, the magazine for Black men.* He swallowed a mouthful of the whisky. It went down real smooth after the first couple of swallows.

"Editor of *Duh Playa*? Why me?" Jack had asked.

"Well, Jack, let's be perfectly honest about this. We haven't had a Black editor of this thing since it came out. We think our readers would welcome a Black editor's touch."

"I'll need *complete* independence."

"Sorry, Jack, that's out of the question. Let's get something straight right from the beginning. The editor of the magazine—Black, White, any color—is simply the editor. I retain the rights of complete control of the content, the layout, the pictures, etc."

"So you just want me to be a front for you?"

"It'll either be you or some other Black guy."

Dirty rotten bastards—he was hip to their game. If the public hated the pictures of the crackhead-ho-nude models with the garter belts, they could blame the Black guy whose name was on the masthead: "editor."

And Ron Wildstock would be looking . . .

And Ron Wildstock will be looking over my shoulder, slobbering to fire me for anything. Whatever. He stared down at the pages on the table. His book *Death Time* was out there now—the real story of how much Iraq fucked a lot of men up. Now he was working on the beginning outline for *Fallujah Fun*, his new book. *I hope they don't put another one of those gruesome fuckin' covers on this one, and it would help a whole lot if I had a chance to correct the galleys.*

Jack shook his head in disgust at the thought of the number of typos he'd marked in *Death Time*. How the hell could they publish something like that? Well, there it was, it was out there, gruesome cover, typos, and all.

Fuck that. Fuck everything. I'll become the first black editor of one of the lousiest black man-oriented magazines in the country. So what? So fuckin' what? Nothing matters any fuckin' way. Drunk again.

Jack tilted the water glass with the Jack Daniels in it up to his lips and slowly swallowed. After he drained the glass, he placed it in a cleared spot on his table-desk, pushed the pages in front of him off to the side, cradled his head in his arms, and passed out. Drunk again.

CHAPTER 9

So What?

"Hey, Harvey, what the fuck is this?" Benton asked. "Some kind of conspiracy?"

"I don't know what you're talking about, Benton," Harvey Dawkins replied.

"Well, let me explain f' God's sake! First, we get Icepick Slim coming in here to accuse us of cooking the books. Then we get Ronald Cummings in here asking for an advance on a book he hasn't even written yet. And now you."

"I'm talking to you about a book cover and promotion. Maybe I could add cookin' the books to this if I thought about it hard enough."

"I don't get it. What's with you guys? If it wasn't for Hollow Daze House, your works wouldn't be in print."

"I don't see anything to be grateful or humble about. If it weren't for us, Hollow Daze House wouldn't be here. It's not a one-way street, Benton; think about it."

"I don't have to think about it. It's a chicken-egg situation—we'll never know which one came first."

"Bullshit, Benton, this is not about chickens and eggs. We came first. In the beginning was the word, remember that."

"Okay, okay already. So now what it is you want us to do?" Benton finally asked.

"The book cover you have on *Time Out* doesn't offer a truthful reflection of what the book is about," Harvey explained.

"It doesn't have to. Book covers are just book covers; they're not supposed to tell you the whole story of what's in the book."

Harvey Dawkins ground his molars together as he thought seriously of beating Benton Marsh down to the floor and then strangling him. After thirty years of studying various martial arts, he knew he could do it easily. He could already see the headlines: "Pissed off writer beats, strangles Hollow Daze House Publishing Company CEO in a dispute about a book cover and book promotion."

"That's the weirdest thing I've ever heard, Benton." Harvey scoffed. "I've never picked up a book that had a cover that didn't give you some idea of what the book is bout."

"Oh, you're talking about that twenty-five-dollar, artsy craftsy, coffee table type things."

Harvey Dawkins deliberately cooled himself out, hip to Benton Marsh's way of talking around things. If he had decided that he wasn't going to give you a straight answer, you could be certain that the conversation was going to chase its own tail.

"Let's put the cover issue on hold for the time being," Benton suggested. "What about promotion?"

"I would like to promote the book—you know, go 'round to the bookstores and sell the book."

"I don't have any objection to that."

"It will mean that I should get some funding," Harvey continued, "a budget of some kind from Hollow Daze."

"Frankly, I can't really see the point of going to the bookstores and all that sort of thing. Your books are selling pretty well."

"If they're selling so well, then why are my royalties so small?" Harvey questioned.

"Here we go again. What's with you guys? Hollow Daze gives an adequate advance and then a percentage from each book sold. I can assure you, my friend, that Hollow Daze is strictly on the up-'n'-up."

Harvey left Benton Marsh's office feeling frustrated, as usual. *No matter how we start off, we always seem to wind up going around and around*, he thought as he left. *And we wind up in the same spot.*

Clay Block stared at the title of the synopsis of Ruuth Morrissey's latest effort: *I Was White, He Was Black*. *Oh God, here we go again*, Clay thought. *What was the other one?* I Was Black, He Was White.

Clay walked around the corner of his desk to peek out of the doorway of his office. He had to make certain Benton or Ron weren't creeping around, trying to catch people doing wrong.

The coast was clear. He stutter-stepped back to his desk, opened the top drawer on the left-hand side, pulled a half-empty fifth of Jack Daniels out, poured himself a half coffee cup of whisky, and sat back down at his desk. *Now if one of these bastards peeks in here, he'll see a man with a coffee mug—nothing wrong with that.*

Clay Block was operating in the delusional world of the drunk. No one with a nose could ignore the sour mash aroma in the room and on Clay's breath, the barely controlled level of his intoxication. He took a hard sip of his drink, adjusted his glasses, and reluctantly started to read *I Was White, He Was Black*.

This story is partially autobiographical, as are most stories. The year is yesterday, but not too very long ago, and the place is the sovereign state of Mississippi.

Clay took another hard sip. *Mississippi—I'm quite familiar with that particular piece of real estate, 'specially 'round Biloxi.*

You couldn't help but notice Ben Jackson. He was the star runnin' back of our small college football team. He was six feet two inches tall in his bare feet and had a body that looked like it was carved out of hard, black coal. And he wasn't just a dumb jock either; the boy had some smarts about him.

Me? I had been crowned Miss Cotton Ball in my freshman year, and it appeared that I was going to be one of the leading candidates for the title of Miss Magnolia Blossom, a highly sought after honor at Jeff Davis Junior College. No one spoke about it openly, but there was an under-the-table understanding that Miss Cotton Ball and Miss Magnolia Blossom had to be White, blonde (if possible), and blue-eyed. It wouldn't hurt if she looked good in a bikini either.

Fortunately, I must say, my gene pool had been real good to me, and I qualified on all cards. Now what happened is this.

Clay Block placed the neatly typed pages on his desk, pushed his glasses up on his forehead, and massaged his bloodshot eyes. "Now what happened is this." That was sort of a Ruuth Morrissey's trademark way of getting into her story. He felt tempted to take a red marker and scribble across the top of the page "Now What Happened Was This." But resisted the temptation, pulled his glasses back down onto his bulb-shaped nose, took another sip of Jack, and read on.

Me and Ben had our lockers in the same corridor. It was like he was at one end, and I was at the other. You have to remember we're not talking of the Mississippi of olden times when we had total segregation. It wasn't against the law for Ben to speak to me or for me to speak to him.

But what we had was like voluntary social segregation—that is to say, White students hung out with White students, and Black students hung out with Black students. During the time I was at Jeff Davis, I never saw any mixed dating or anything like that.

So now what happened was this. One afternoon I happened to be getting something out of my locker, and nobody was in the corridor but me and Ben Jackson—he down there at that end, and me down here at my end. I had just got my stuff from the bottom of my locker as he was passing by. He said to me, in a real low, sexy voice, "You real cute, Suzy Belle. You know that?"

"You're kinda cute yourself, Ben Jackson," I replied. Lord only knows what made me say that. But of course, it was the truth. Ben Jackson was more than cute; he was fine. I mean fine.

That was the way it started off. He would speak to me and say something funny or cute when nobody was around. And I got to doing the same thing. And then one day, one late afternoon, never will forget it. I was digging 'round in my locker looking for something, and Ben came up behind me, reached around, and cupped both of my breasts in his big ol' hands. "I been wantin' to do that for a long time," he whispered.

He made me feel like I was gonna melt on the spot. I couldn't think of nothing to do but turn around and kiss his big ol' lips hard as I could. And that's where it was when my locker mate, my best friend, Donna Lee Jenkins, came to the locker. Ben had walked on down the corridor.

"Suzy Belle," Donna whispered to me, "I saw y'all. Don't worry, I ain't gonna tell nobody, I'm your friend."

It was right there, right at that particular moment that the realization really hit me—I'm White, and he is Black. And thusly the story begins.

Clay Block pushed his glasses back up onto his forehead. It wasn't much different from her other stuff, inventory was low, and it was a proven fact that Ruuth Morrissey's stuff was selling well. He took a long sip of his drink and scribbled a memo to Benton Marsh:

"Morrissey's latest—*I Was White, He Was Black*—is in her typical vein. As you know, she has an audience, so I would think this one is okay."

What the fuck, he thought.

Ron Wildstock drummed his fingers on the edge of his desk. *Where is he? I called for this asshole fifteen minutes ago. How long does it take to walk down the hall?* A timid tap, tap, tap on the door signaled Jack Mozel's arrival.

"C'mon in!" Ron greeted him.

Jack made a tentative entry, dark circles under his eyes from a half-soused night spent writing his latest novel, trying to avoid having his usual Iraqi nightmare, and figuring out a way to bring out another issue of *Duh Playa*.

He had discovered some interesting perks connected to being the editor of the soft porn magazine. Number one, he was receiving a regular paycheck for the first time in years.

Number two, he had access to a Rolodex full of black women who were willing to sleep with the editor of *Duh Playa* just for the chance to appear in the magazine. Amazing.

The downside was his relationship with Ron Wildstock, the power behind the throne.

"Have a seat, Jack," Ron said. "I wanna talk to you about the last issue of *Duh Playa*."

Uh-oh. Jack perched on the edge of the low, black, fake leather chair in front of Wildstock's desk. He was almost certain that Wildstock had deliberately found a low-bottomed chair that he could look down on from his elevated seat behind his desk. Talk about insecure Napoleonic types.

The five feet seven Wildstock sat on his high seat behind his desk. At five feet eleven, Jack Mozel's shoulders barely came up to Wildstock's desktop. Wildstock held up the latest issue of *Duh Playa*.

"Okay, Jack, you wanna explain this?" Ron began.

"Explain what?"

"Explain why you took advantage of my absence to publish this—to put all of this crap in *Duh Playa*."

Jack Mozel sat up a little straighter, genuinely puzzled. *What the hell is this guy talking about?* Ron Wildstock flipped through the pages of the magazine, a disgusted look distorting his features.

"Look at this! An article about some ol' Black guy named Paul Robeson. What the hell do our readers care about a fuckin' commie from yesterday? And this shit about 'the roles that African American actresses should've played in Hollywood, starting with Cleopatra.' Who gives a shit about that?

"And this long piece of junk about Cuban cigars and rum. We're dealing with beer drinkers and cigarette smokers here. But worst of all, look at this fucked up cover."

Mozel stared at the gorgeous Ethiopian woman on the cover of the sixth edition of *Duh Playa*. *Let me play this cool*, he thought to himself.

He recognized immediately that three biggies were at stake: his regular paycheck, his sexual access to a collection of willing Black females, and the possibility that Hollow Daze Publishing Company might decide not to publish any more of his *Death* books. *Maybe I can finesse my way past Ron Wildstock's bullshit. I have to.*

"Uh, Ron, what seems to be the problem? What're you upset about?" Jack asked calmly.

He remained cool as he watched Ron Wildstock's face go from a sourdough pasty to a steamed lobster red, complete with popped out veins in the neck and temple areas.

"What seems to be the fuckin' problem?! I'll tell you what the fuckin' problem is—in detail. You got a couple of minutes?"

Jack nodded yes, ignoring Wildstock's sarcasm. *The best thing to do is humor this li'l ol' crazy ass, racist bastard.*

"Good. Glad you can accommodate me. Let me start with this cover."

"Her name is Miriam Kebede, Miss Ethiopia-America of 2010. We were lucky to be able to grab her for the cover," Jack stated.

"You were lucky?!" Wildstock exploded. "You were lucky?! No, mister, you were not lucky! You were arrogant! You went against one of my cardinal rules for our cover girls.

"We do not have any 'pretty girls' on the cover of *Duh Playa*. You gotta remember, pal, the brothers are not into 'pretty,' they're into 'accessible.'

"We don't wanna have some poor schmuck look at the cover of this magazine and see a chick who looks unapproachable. I thought I had made that quite clear to you when you came aboard, long before I took off for the Frankfurt Book Fair."

Jack Mozel did a semibow in his chair and plastered a shit-eating grin on his face. He felt it was the most diplomatic thing to do.

"So what happens? I go to the Fair to promote our Hollow Daze House books—your books, Jack Mozel—and what do you do?

"What do you do while I'm overseas hustlin' my butt off for the likes of you? You bring out an issue of *Duh Playa* that is the complete antithesis of what this magazine is all about!"

Jack winced. "Antithesis of what this magazine is all about." What the hell did that mean? He decided to take a loser's gamble.

"Uh, maybe I'm a li'l bit confused here, Ron. If this latest issue of an African American soft porn mag—"

"It's a Black thang, Jack, a Black thang. I thought we had leveled that out during our first story conference."

Jack tried to conceal the irritation he felt. "A Black thang?" Who in the hell was Ron Wildstock to decide what a "Black thang" was?

"Okay, it's a 'Black thang,'" Jack continued. "In any case, starting with the beautiful Miriam Kebede—"

"I hate seeing this fuckin' foreigner on the cover of our Black American magazine!"

Jack couldn't conceal his puzzled look. *What the hell was foreign about an Ethiopian model on the cover of an African American soft porn magazine? 'Specially one that featured nude African American women only. And what made Miriam Kebede unapproachable? The fact that she was beautiful? Weren't brothers drawn to beautiful women?*

"Sorry, Ron, maybe I'm missing something here. What's wrong with having a beautiful African woman on the cover of a magazine being marketed to African American males?"

Ron Wildstock's mean-spirited expression reached a number of levels. *Why can't you fuckin' understand what I'm saying?* Ron silently wondered. *What is the problem here?*

"Jack, let me give it to you slowly. *Duh Playa* is aimed at a bunch of African American men—dudes of a certain intellectual class, to put it bluntly—and I can assure you that they would rather see one of their own on the front of *Duh Playa* rather than some weird-ass, exotic-looking broad. You know what I'm sayin'?"

Jack nodded meekly. He had decided to fall in line with Ron Wildstock's twisted logic, because he wasn't prepared to cut his regular paycheck off, didn't want to lose access to a collection of willing females, and was afraid that if he pushed back too hard, the Hollow Daze House outlet would be closed to him.

"Uh yeah, Ron, I hear you, man. I hear you," Jack said. "What happened was that we, uh, had set up a shoot for Monique LaTush, and for some reason, at the last minute she couldn't make it."

"Oh yes, Monique LaTush—I just love that Black bitch!"

Jack Mozel took a deep breath and swallowed his pride. *Be cool, brother. Be cool. . . . This will be all over in a few minutes.*

"Yeah, Monique is fine, no doubt about that," Jack agreed. "Well, anyway, to make a long story short, our photographer said that he knew this Ethiopian sister about fifteen minutes away who would die to be on the cover of *Duh Playa*."

"So that's how you wound up with 'Madam Exotique,' huh?"

"That's what happened."

"Well, see that it doesn't happen again."

Jack ground his molars, tightened his sphincters, and stared down at some invisible object between his feet.

"Like I said, Ron—"

"Yeah, yeah, I know what you said—it was the photographer's choice. Well, get this through your nappy, thick skull, Jack: you're the fuckin' editor of *Duh Playa*, and we're paying *you* to put the right chick on the cover every month. Dig? We're paying *you*, pal, to do a job. We're not paying the photographers to do your work.

"Incidentally, what about Monique? You had a chance to crack a piece of that off yet? After the second interview I had with her, I jammed my cock down that Black bitch's—"

In that moment, the reddish darkness that Jack Mozel had seen when he killed his first human being up close in Iraq dropped down on him. He jumped across Ron Wildstock's desk and landed on his chest. It took him two quick movements to get behind Wildstock and hammerlock his head and twist until he heard the snap that told him that he had broken his neck.

It was at that moment that he realized that someone was screaming—*he* was screaming. "I won't let you treat me like a fuckin' dog, Wildstock! I won't let you talk to me like a dog, Wildstock! Do you hear me?! Do you hear me, you racist-ass motherfucker you?!"

CHAPTER 10

The Players Do Not Play

The building had to be evacuated, and eight muscular policemen had to taser and subdue Jack Mozel. Benton Marsh, Clay Block, and the staff of Hollow Daze Publishing House formed an aisle for the police to drag Jack Mozel through, kicking, screaming, and foaming from the mouth.

"I'm a fuckin' vet! I've killed motherfuckers! I will not allow y'all to disrespect me! I hate all you motherfuckers! I hate every goddamned one of you! I hate y'all!"

He was still screaming after they stuffed him into the backseat of a patrol car and drove away. Several of the secretaries were obviously in a state of shock. Benton was sympathetic, up to a point.

"Awright everybody! The show is over. Let's get back to work," he ordered. "I'm not paying you guys to hang around out here!"

Clay Block was the first to go back into the building to get back to the almost empty bottle of Jack Daniels in the upper-left drawer of his desk. *Poor Ron, what a terrible way to go—to have somebody break your neck. Poor Jack, what made you go off like that?* he pondered.

The daily newspapers gave the story a front-page column: "Demented editor of *Duh Playa* magazine goes postal on his boss, motivation for the homicide has not been determined."

Mel Grant read the details before passing the newspaper to Alice W. Hiker, his overnight weekend guest.

"Alice, this is one of your people, isn't it?"

She scribbled a few more words on her legal pad before reaching for the newspaper. She read the leading paragraphs twice before lowering the paper.

"Wow! Jack finally went off."

"Jack Mozel? That's the guy who broke the dude's neck. Did you know him?" Mel asked.

"I'd have to say not directly, but in a roundabout way. I think we—all of the Big Six, as someone once labeled us—know each other: Jack Mozel, Icepick Slim, Ronald Cummins, Harvey Dawkins, Ruuth Morrissey (the White girl who wants to be Black), and myself.

"A couple of years ago, a White reporter did a big spread about us in *Big Town Today*, about how we had basically made Hollow Daze House a success story. Ruuth Morrissey was thrilled to death to be accidentally identified as a Black writer."

Alice W. Hiker read the rest of the article and folded the paper in four neat squares after she finished. She and Mel Grant sprawled out on the wooden deck of his Ladera Heights condo, casually studying Los Angeles, looking north through the hazy clouds of a September day.

Alice smiled and reached over to feel Mel's hand—the man in the yellow suit.

"Mel, you know something?"

"What's that, sweetheart?" he asked.

"I'm at that point in this li'l novel I'm writing about us where I have to explain—offer some motivation for the man in the yellow suit."

"And then what? *The Man in the Ivory-White Suit, The Man in the Mint-Green Suit, The Man—*"

"I know, I know. You have all of those, but it's that canary-yellow suit that first seduced me."

"Here, come sit beside me, and I'll give you the yellow-suit rundown."

She slipped under his left arm, and she thought about how well they fit together. He tilted her face up to his for a series of little kisses from the bridge of her nose to both eyes. *I love his tenderness, his sense of humor*, she thought.

"Funny you should ask me about the suit," he said. "I was wondering when you would get around to it."

"Just goes to show you how the curious mind works. After you told me about coming here from Atlanta a couple of years ago, your divorce from that dreadful woman down there—"

"Thank God we didn't have any kids."

"About your successful contracting business, I thought you were in the cocaine trade and not the building trade at first. Till you brought me into this gorgeous place you built."

"I'm glad you like it," he spoke seriously.

"I love it. It all fell into place after I got to know you a little bit."

They exchanged a deep, probing kiss.

"Everything but the yellow suit," she continued.

"That's my Alice, persistent as water. Well, here's the way it happened," Mel began. "I got lucky the first three months after I arrived in Los Angeles. I had the capital from the sellout of my assets in Atlanta; I'm a hard worker, as you know, and the minute I figured out how the business was done here, I was off 'n' runnin'."

"I don't have to remind you of how I lucked up on this place, half finished, just sitting here waiting for me."

"The yellow suit?"

"I'm almost there—ha-ha. Well, let me put it this way—man does not live by bread alone. After a couple of years, I had a few bucks in the bank, business was picking up steadily, but I didn't have anybody to share my life with. Must be the Cancerian in me. I've already named names."

"And so have I," Alice noted.

"So I don't have to hide that section of my LA life. The problem that I was having had to do with the kind of dude I am, basically. I was looking for someone—I was looking for you—but I didn't know what shape or size you would come in. Meanwhile, I had some good buddies tell me, 'Hey, man, this is LA. If you want to meet the fly girls, you've got to do something about your wardrobe.' One of them went shopping with me, and that's how I wound up with the yellow suit, the ivory suit—all of 'em. My friends had convinced me that the most dynamic ladies wanted a 'bad boy,' a 'playa.' So that's the front I put on. As you know, it wasn't something that I was ever completely comfortable with."

They snuggled closer together. She stroked the side of his face. She had been totally surprised after that afternoon in the Blues Room to be invited to go on a picnic in Griffith Park the following weekend—a picnic of catered Japanese goodies in Griffith Park and, after that, visits to the Los Angeles County Museum of Art and hip trips to ethnic festivals around and about.

"Don't you just love to see how the other people see things, what they eat, what they think is important?"

They had spent weekends at the Thai Town Festival on Western and Hollywood Boulevard, the Cuban Fiesta and the Lotus Blossom Festival in Echo Park, the Day of the Drum at the Watts Towers Arts Center in Watts, the Greek Festival on Pico and Normandie, the Pan-African Film Festival, the African Market Place, and in between times, trips to the International Music Festival in Ojai and the San Francisco Jazz Festival.

"So now I know how the yellow suit came into being," Alice concluded.

"Looks like the brother knew what he was talking about."

"Well now, Mr. Grant, I would have to say that I think it was about much more than your yellow suit."

"I hope so. Why don't we go inside and have a couple of chicken salad sandwiches for lunch?" Mel suggested.

"We had lunch about forty-five minutes ago."

"Did we have dessert?" he asked with a suggestive tone in his voice. She stood and gently pulled him up, and they strolled into the house with their arms linked around each other's waists.

Two Years Later

"Mark! Dammit! Are you listening to me?!"

"I hear you, Dad, but I don't know if I'm *listening* to you."

"What the hell does that mean?"

"It means just what I said."

Benton Marsh felt a great urge to throw his cup of coffee across the kitchen table at his son but cancelled out the urge.

Why should I break a perfectly good coffee cup on him? He decided to cool his anger out and become a bit more diplomatic.

"Okay, Mark, you hear me. Good. Maybe that's all you need to do right now. What I'm trying to make you understand is very simple. You're twenty-nine years old, and I want to bring you into the biz."

"The biz"—that would strike the right chord. Sounds like a word he can relate to. Benton rushed on to the central theme of Mark's appeal.

"Mark, I'm not getting any younger, and I need you," Benton continued. "I need someone in this thing with me, someone I can trust, someone I know who will take care of my back. The money is there, Mark, believe me; the money is there. We got the publishing house, first off, the porno videos, investments in real estate, high earning stocks."

Mark Marsh curled his lips down with contempt. "So what the fuck makes you think I wanna get involved with all that crap?"

"Do you have to use profanity, Mark? Do you have to?"

"No, Dad, I don't have to fuckin' use profanity, but I'm usin' it, so fuckin' what?" Mark snapped back.

Control yourself, control yourself, control yourself . . . he's your son. "Okay, so you want to use profanity, but I'd like to remind you that you're sitting in exactly the same chair that your mother used to sit in, God rest her soul."

"So what the fuck is that supposed to mean? You think she's gonna come back and fuckin' haunt me or somethin'?"

"Why can't you have a little more respect?" Benton asked.

"Respect for what? For you? Why should I have respect for you?!"

"Because I'm your father, dammit!"

"If that's what you wanna call yourself. I can't really think of you as a father; you've always been the guy who was on his way to the next meeting, on his way to make the next buck. You've never been a father. Fathers take their sons to the zoo, for walks in the park, come to see them play soccer on Saturday afternoons.

"Fathers don't park their sons in fucked-up military academies for years just to get them out of the way."

"Awright, you want to go there, huh? You want to try to hit below the belt, huh? Well, let me tell you—there are thousands, maybe millions, of kids out there who would've welcomed the kind of privileged upbringing you had. You're not going to blame me for your drug addictions," Benton began. "Look at you. You're twenty-nine years old, never done an honest day's work in your life, never done anything but smoke dope, shoot dope, sell dope. You oughta take a good look at yourself. Who in the world would hire somebody with those gruesome-looking tattoos on your face and neck?

"Now here I am, your father, whether you like it or not, offering you a chance to put all of that negative stuff behind you. I'm offering you a chance to turn your miserable life around. You've been out of prison two weeks, and you're back on the pipe again already. You can't fool me; I know a junky when I see one."

"Call me any fuckin' thing you wanna call me," Mark responded. "I don't care."

Benton stared at the hurt expression that flitted across his son's face. It was just a moment, but he could recall the expression from another time. A coyote had snuck into the back area of their Mandeville Canyon home and trotted away with Mark's pet rabbit in his long snout.

"Don't worry, Mark. We'll get you another one."

"You can't replace Freddy, Dad. I loved that rabbit."

"We'll buy you another one, honey. You'll love it just as much."

"No, Mom, I'll never love another one like that one. You can't substitute things you love."

Benton saw an opening, maybe the expression that flitted across his son's face was a small window to a soft spot. He decided to go at it.

"Mark, look, what purpose does it serve for us to be going at each other like this? Why don't you take a week or so to think about my offer? I'd bring you in as my special assistant, give you a decent salary—"

Mark seemed to explode.

"I don't want to follow in your fuckin' footsteps, Dad! Don't you get it?! I don't want to be dealin' with a fuckin' bunch of nigger writers. Okay? I don't want to be forced to listen to all of their bitchin' 'n' complainin'. Isn't that what you've been talkin' about for years?!

"I don't want to get my fuckin' neck broken by some outta control nigger like your partner Ron Wildstock."

Benton stared at his son's contorted expression, made even more vicious looking by the grotesque tattoos.

"Mark, what the hell is wrong with you?! I've never taught you to hate anybody. Where did you get this racist nonsense from?"

Mark Marsh ripped his shirt open to expose a cluster of swastikas around his navel. "I'm a bona fide, certified member of the White Flower Committee. We hate niggers, and we hate White people who don't love White people. You hate niggers too, Dad. The only difference between me and you is that you're a closet racist, and I'm up front about it.

"You want to make your money off exploitin' the niggers, and I don't want to have a fuckin' thing to do with them."

Benton Marsh took careful aim before he smashed his coffee cup against his son's forehead. Mark wiped the coffee off of his face.

"You know something?" Mark ground the words out as he spoke. "You know somethin'? If you weren't my fuckin' father, I'd fuck you up."

"Get out of here and don't ever show your ugly face again."

Mark shuffled away from the table without a backward glance.

CHAPTER 11

The Final Blow—

The Funeral of Icepick Slim

The word came over the "jungle telegraph" two whole days prior to the official obituary notice that appeared in the *Los Angeles Times*: "Robert Brewster, aka Icepick Slim, author of the street corner classic *Pimpin'*, died of congestive heart failure at his home on Thursday. Icepick Slim leaves a brother and sister in Chicago."

Icepick Slim, the legend, was discussed, argued about, and toasted, but not mourned.

"That motherfucker shoulda been dead years ago."

"I ain't gonna believe his ass is dead till I look down on his face in the casket."

"The newspaper say he died of a 'congestive heart failure.' I think it was that coke that killed him. I remember about ten years ago he had to have surgery done to repair the lining in his nose. He had tooted so much blow he had worn the lining in his nose out."

"Yeah, he was known to love two things—coke snortin' and pimpin'."

"Yes indeed, he was a hard pimpin' motherfucker, no doubt about that."

"I say he pimped his ass to death."

"Thought he gave up pimpin'?"

"Could you give up breathin'?"

"Bet we gonna have some lost hoes out there tonight."

"Yeah, I can just see 'em goin' 'round askin', 'Where Daddy at? Where Daddy done gone?'"

It took Benton Marsh exactly two minutes to come up with an idea after reading about Icepick Slim's death in the morning paper. He stomped through the reception area of his office, a wicked gleam in his eyes, the *LA Times* tucked under his arm.

"'Mornin', Mr. Marsh."

"'Mornin', Carolyn. Clay come in yet?"

"Not yet."

Benton glanced up at the clock above the receptionist's head. It was 9:45 a.m., and Benton realized he'd have to chew Clay's ass out again. *Who the hell does he think he is, coming in later than the boss?*

Benton hung his sports coat and black fedora on the coat rack in the corner, eased himself into the seat behind his neatly arranged desk, and spread the obituary open in front of him.

Robert Brewster, aka Icepick Slim, author of the street corner classic *Pimpin'*, died of congestive heart failure at his home on Thursday. Icepick Slim leaves as brother and sister in Chicago.

Benton heard a timid tap, tap on the door. Clay Block had finally arrived. "Come in, Clay," he called.

Clay Block slunk into Benton's office, fully prepared to accept the ass chewing he knew he was about to receive.

"Uh, you wanted to see me, Benton?"

"Yeah, glad you could finally make it. As you know, the employees, even you, Clay, are expected to be here at nine o'clock."

"Sorry, Benton, the traffic—"

"Yeah, yeah, yeah, the traffic. Save it. Sit down. I got a proposition to make to you. You interested in making a few extra grand a year?"

Clay almost missed the set as he stared at Benton's mouth and perched on the edge.

"A few extra grand a year? Is that what you said?"

"Read my lips. That's what I'm saying—a few extra grand a year," Benton repeated.

Clay Block's face lit up. What the hell was happening here? Benton Marsh offering him a raise? Maybe it was all falling into place. Paul's return to his arms after many months of being *"out there."*

"Clay, do you still love me?"

"You know I do, Paul. You know I do."

Their lovemaking to celebrate his lover's return had intensity to it that Clay had never experienced before. And now, stingy-stingy Benton Marsh was offering him a raise.

"Well?"

"Uh, yes, of course I'd be very happy to accept a few extra grand a year."

"Good. I didn't think you would refuse my offer. Have you read today's paper?" Benton asked.

"Uh no, not yet."

"Icepick Slim kicked the bucket a couple of days ago. His obituary is in today's paper."

"Oh, sorry to hear that. He wasn't very old, was he? About sixty or so. What was the cause of—"

"Heart failure. Now, my question to you as the chief editor here is this: Did this guy die and leave four or five manuscripts with you? With Hollow Daze? Manuscripts that you had edited, just waiting to be published?"

"No, not that I can think of."

Benton placed his elbows on his desk and leaned toward his editor.

"Clay, clear the cobwebs away from your brain and listen to me carefully, 'cause I'm not going to repeat myself. Did Robert Brewster, aka Icepick Slim, author of the best-selling street corner classic, *Pimpin'*, die and leave four or five about-to-be-published manuscripts with you? With Hollow Daze House Publishing Company?"

Oh my God, what is this ghoul asking me to do? Clay thought. "As a matter of fact, he did leave four manuscripts with us." Clay spoke in a low, resigned voice.

"As a matter of fact, he left *five* manuscripts with us—*five*, Clay, *five*. As his primary editor, I'm sure you're completely familiar with his writing style. Correct?"

"Yes, I'm familiar—"

"Great. Now we don't want to glut the Icepick Slim market, but we would like to see his next book on the shelves—let's say, four months from now. What's the title of the book, Clay?"

Clay Block closed his eyes for a hot minute, trying to blot the scene out of his mind.

"The title?"

"Yes, the title of the next book, Clay. The book that we are going to publish posthumously, that's going to fatten your salary by a few grand."

"How many grand?"

Benton's eyes darted from Clay's suddenly bold question to the window, to the uncluttered top of his desk, back to Clay's question.

"We'll have to work that out."

"I won't be able to start working/editing *Big Time Charlie* until we get that little detail worked out," Clay noted.

Clay suddenly felt an instant rush of perspiration under his armpits, and he placed both hands on his knees to keep them from shaking. Benton looked irritated.

"Clay, I don't think I have to tell you that time is of the essence in a situation like this."

"I know, Benton, I know."

Benton Marsh leaned back in his seat, tented his fingers under his chin, and stared at Clay Block. *You little worm, you. I oughta kick your ass out of here. But who else knows the Icepick style? Who else could I call on to get the job done? Lots of money to be made off of a few more Icepick Slim books, published after his death.*

"Okay, Clay, let's say three grand."

"Let's say five grand," Clay countered.

"Five grand, huh?"

"Yeah, five grand."

Benton drummed on the edge of his desk. He was feeling threatened, pissed. The nerve of this drunk bastard.

"Awright, Clay, five grand it is." He finally agreed.

"Good. I'll have my attorney draw up a contract."

"We can't put any kind of deal like this in a contract. You know better than that."

"Of course. The contract will simply stipulate that you are granting me a bonus of five grand for each of the Icepick books I'll be editing."

"What the hell are you talking about?!" Benton howled. "Five grand per book?! I thought you meant five grand for all five!"

Clay Block stood up slowly. His knees felt a little wobbly, and he felt a great urge to get to his desk for a morning hit on his new bottle of Jack, but he was feeling a surge of pride in being able to negotiate with mighty Benton Marsh from a position of strength.

"I want five grand for each book, Benton. I don't have to tell you that I'll be doing an awful lot of work to 'edit' *Big Time Charlie, Sally Mae, The Real Game, Icepick's Secrets,* and *Slim's Nose Candy.*"

Benton couldn't control his sudden excitement. "Those are the titles!? Those are the titles?!"

"Well, for now, off the top of my head. I may change the titles, but for now, those are the titles," Clay confirmed.

Benton cooled his sudden excitement down. "Awright, Clay, you get your guy to do the contract, and I'll have my guy look it over."

"Fair enough. Well, time for me to get to my desk."

Benton Marsh watched Clay Block weave his way to the door.

"Oh, Clay, don't forget," Benton called after him. "The work day starts at nine o'clock around here."

Clay Block opened the door and turned back to reply. "Thanks for that info, Benton. Thanks a lot."

Benton slumped down into his chair, a sarcastic smile lurking on his lips. *Five grand a book? No problem. Wonder where this asshole got the nerve to butt heads with me?*

Some people were still talking about Icepick Slim's funeral. Hundreds, some say thousands, filed past his open casket at the funeral home on Crenshaw. The "stars" of the hour were a chartered busload of hoes from New York City.

"We started talkin' about it, and then somebody suggested that we should pay our respects."

"Yeah, that's why we came. We wanted to show our respect. You know what I'm sayin'?"

The hoes were eclipsed by the fifty pimps who came to the funeral—legends of the game. Pimps like Waikiki Willie from Honolulu, Frisco Frank, Mr. Lord Money from New York, and others dazzled the afternoon service with their diamonds, gold, expensive cars, and outrageous garments.

Rev. Harry Horner, an ex-pimp himself, gave an elegant witness and testimonial for Icepick Slim. Reverend Horner's mahogany-grained voice was broadcast over a loudspeaker to those who couldn't get a seat inside the two-thousand-seat auditorium.

"We have gathered here today," the good reverend announced, "to pay our respect to Mr. Robert Brewster, better known to most of y'all as Icepick Slim."

The pimps, would-be pimps, minor league playas, and bona fide hos took a detailed look at Reverend Horner's James Brown hairdo, the pure gold cross hanging on his chest, the ice-cream colored, double-breasted suit, the diamonds on his fingers and thumbs, the $2,500 handmade gators on his well-pedicured feet. He was one of them; he was the right man for the job.

"I'm not gonna stand up here 'n' rant 'n' rave all day, because y'all got busy schedules—I know that. And I know that Pick would not have wanted me to do a lot of pontificatin'."

The audience shared a hip, collective laugh. They were relieved they could be back on the track in a couple of hours.

"First off, let me say this: Icepick Slim came to be who he was the hard way. I'm stressin' this point, because there are some among us who might think that he inherited his position from his daddy or that somebody crowned him the Prince of Pimps. I was a close friend of Icepick Slim, and I can tell you straight up that he had to put in some work to get to where he got."

Reverend Horner paused to rub an imaginary speck of dust off of his right eyelid, carefully tilting his right pinky diamond ring of many carats to catch a shaft of sunlight streaming through the Technicolored windows.

"There were hard, cold days for Icepick—days when he didn't know who was goin' to bring his money in, days and nights when he didn't know who was goin' to pay for his car, who was goin' to stay on the job or who was goin' to flee. After all, the name of the game is still cop and blow. Some might say—cop, and they go."

A collection of amens erupted form the pimps in the second and third rows. Reverend Horner smiled and pulled a snow-white hanky out of his breast pocket to wipe nonexistent beads of sweat from his smooth brow.

"Now I, unlike some other men of the cloth, would be the last one to criticize or condemn Icepick Slim's lifestyle, the way he earned his daily bread. To those who would be critical, I would simply say, 'He who is without a sin should be the first to toss a stone.' But I would also like to remind y'all that some of those who *say* they are without sin are livin' in glass houses. And that's not a real good thang. Can I hear an amen from the church?!"

The free-thinking assembly showed their appreciation of Reverend Horner's remarks by calling out, "I heard that!" "Yeah, reverend, you got that right." "I'll second that! Amen!" Reverend Horner, caught in the moment, did a careful origami folding of his breast pocket hanky before carefully stuffing it back into his breast pocket.

"Oh yes! Icepick Slim had to put in some work to get to where he got! Some would agree that what he did come easy. That is *not* correct. *What* he did and the *way* he did it made it seem easy, but it was never easy. I can recall many days when he would come to me with some of his problems.

"'Harry,' he said to me. I was just plain ol' Harry Horner on the corner at that time." Reverend Horner paused to double wink at the foxy little beige-skinned hoe in the first row, the one with the cleavage cut almost to her jeweled belly button.

"'Harry,' he said to me, 'I've been thinkin' hard about gettin' out of the game.'

"'But why, Pick? The rumor has been goin' around that you made more than the president last year.' He smiled. I'll always remember that smile. It was kinda sad.

"'Oh, don't get me wrong, Harry, it ain't about the money. The money is comin' in real good.

"'Then what's the problem?' I asked him.

"'It's got to do with the outrageous hours I'm keeping. Sometimes I may not get more than four hours sleep in three days 'cause I'm always on the go, got things to do. Some people think I do coke 'cause I love it. That's not true. I do it 'cause it's the best way for me to remain alert.

"'I don't have a set time to eat. I may be havin' dinner at nine thirty in the morning and breakfast at midnight. I don't like that, because it keeps me with indigestion all the time, not to mention constipation and heartburn.

"'I turned fifty a week ago, and I was dealin' with so many things I forgot about it. If it hadn't been for one of the members of my entourage '—that's what he called his stable, an entourage—' if it hadn't been for Bebe, I would've forgotten about my own birthday.

"'Stress is what I'm talkin' about, Harry, stress. Every time I turn around I have more stress to deal with. Let me just give you three examples: I went to New York on business last month, and on my way back—you know how much I like to drive—I managed to pluck this ripe li'l piece of fruit off of a tree somewhere in Iowa or maybe it was Indiana. "Oh please take me with you, Mr. Icepick, please, please, please. I wanna get outta this li'l ol' place. I'm tired of milkin' cows and being forced to jack my daddy and my two brothers off all the time. Oh please, please, please," she begged.

'What could I do? I felt like a missionary of Pimpdom who had been called upon to save this voluptuous young blonde girl's body and soul. The only problem, which I didn't find out till weeks later, is that this five-eight, 38-24-38, blue-eyed money magnet was only eighteen years old.

'If it hadn't been for Attorney Cockburne, I would've had that Mann Act on my back like an eight hundred-pound Congolese gorilla. It was really touch 'n' go there for a few months, but we beat the rap. Like I said, if it hadn't been for Cockburne, I would be doin' some serious time for transporting an underage female across state lines for immoral purposes. I can't remember what kind of mumbo jumbo he did, and I don't really give a shit. All I know is that he got me off.

'Example number two coming right up. Three members of my entourage started behavin' rebelliously—you know, answering me back in the wrong tone of voice, throwin' my money on the bed instead of putting it in the upper-right hand drawer of my night table, the way they had been instructed to do.

'One of them actually had nerve enough to try to conceal some of my earnings in her private parts—or, or should I say, tried to conceal my cut in her cunt? I was so distracted, doin' a half dozen other things, that I didn't notice what was happening at first. And then it dawned on me that I had a full-scale rebellion on my hands.

'It took a full week to quell the rebellion, to get things back in order. I had to give number one an extremely serious ass kickin', for starters. That was to let all of the members of my entourage know that there was a certain etiquette to be followed when my money was presented to me. I stripped the other two rebels buck nekkid and kept them in the bathroom on cornbread and water for two days and nights. Why cornbread? 'Cause I've always liked cornbread.

'Stress, Harry, stress. I've had a bad case of insomnia for the past month. I think I need to think of another line of work.'"

Reverend Horner gazed from one shocked pimp face to another.

"Yes, brothers 'n' sisters, that's the buck nekkid, honest-to-God truth. The incomparable Icepick Slim was actually thinkin' about goin' into another field of endeavor, but luckily, he talked to me first. And I'm pleased to say I helped him out.

"I made him understand that he was a unique figure, that he was a sterling role model for many of us, and it would demoralize the rank and file if he threw up his hands and walked away from the game. 'What will happen to your entourage?' I asked him. 'Who will they have to go to for guidance? What will they do with all of that excess money they make?'

"Fortunately, I'm pleased to say, Icepick Slim listened to me and went on to greater heights. I must also take credit for encouragin' him to get off into yoga, Tai Chi, healthy eatin', and meditational walkin'.

"He liked what I laid on him so much he encouraged his entourage to get into it. Do we have any members of Icepick Slim's entourage in the house?

"Ah yes, those twelve gorgeous ladies right there on the left side. Please, ladies, stand up."

Necks and shoulders twisted and heads swiveled to take a good look at the entourage that Icepick Slim had left behind. Appreciative comments were exchanged from pimp to pimp.

"As you can easily see, fresh fruits, veggies, and meditational walkin' can do wonders for the human body. I thank you, ladies.

Please be seated. Now then, to wind this up. I gave Pick some good advice, and he took it a step further. He started writin' to make creative use of his insomnia, and as you all know, he gave us a masterpiece called *Pimpin'*.

"In addition, I might add, he gave me some good advice too. 'Harry, you're too good to be out here holdin' up this corner, man, you oughta become a minister.' And that's exactly what I became as y'all can see. It took me two long years of online study at the Southwestern University of Divine Action to get my diploma, but I have to say—it was worth it.

"At this time I'm gonna invite you brothers 'n' sisters to line up, starting with the twelve gorgeous ladies on the left side, for a final viewing of our friend Icepick Slim. I'm goin' to suggest, for those who are inclined to feel sad about the death of a loved one, that you think a different way as you look down upon the peaceful expression of this man.

"I want you to think about how happy Icepick Slim is right now, surrounded by a new entourage of beautiful angels.

"Yea verily."

CHAPTER 12

Literary Impersonations

Ronald Cummins, three years later—*Daddy Smooth on a Rampage*.

Clay Block strolled over to the decanter on the top of the bookcase in his redecorated office, poured himself a generous three fingers of Jack Daniels, and strolled back to his desk. He stared at the picture of his lover Paul that hung in a frame on the back of the door, the face of his beloved, so he could look at it whenever he closed the door of his office.

"Benton, I must have a door for my office. I can't sit up in there 'editing' Icepick Slim's books, without a door on the hinges."

"Okay, Clay, if you want privacy, you'll get a door," Benton had agreed.

Clay sipped his drink. Life couldn't be sweeter. He felt like celebrating. *Maybe I'll take Paul out to dinner tonight*, he thought.

Five Icepick Slim novels in two and a half years: *Big Time Charlie, Sally Mae, The Real Game, Icepick's Secrets*, and *Slim's Nose Candy*. He had driven himself to write in the Icepick Slim style, to grind the works out. No one questioned the odd circumstances of books being issued by Hollow Daze House after Icepick Slim's death.

"Icepick was a very prolific author," Benton had explained. "We had to stockpile some of his books to prevent his titles from competing for the same dollars."

It was Benton's job to do the RP spin whenever it was needed and Clay Block's job to create the "stockpiled" books. Clay took another

90

hit of Jack, loving the warmth that curled up in his stomach as the hard, smooth liquor slid down. *Think I'll take Paul to the reservation with me this summer if he wants to go—time for some more Native American folktales.*

Clay ignored the phone ringing on his desk for a few rings. *Maybe it's Paul.* He snatched the phone up.

"Yes?"

"Clay, come to my office. I need to talk with you."

"Be there in a half hour, Benton," he responded. "I'm working on something."

Clay Block smiled as he heard Benton Marsh slam his phone down. *What am I supposed to do? You call me like I'm a little puppy, and I'm supposed to run to your office? Fuck you, Benton Marsh.*

Twenty-eight minutes later, properly stoked, Clay made his way through the corridor of doorless offices to his boss's office. The secretaries, the people in the art design department, and Carolyn the receptionist all looked up at Clay as he wobbled past. They had all taken note over the past few years, of the change in the relationship between Benton Marsh and his editor, Clay Block. Clay wasn't more sober, but he was obviously more assertive, more independent acting. Carolyn Price, the short, dark-skinned receptionist, was the only one who knew the reason why Clay was able to puff his chest out a bit, to act more assertive, because she was the one who typed Clay Block's manuscripts.

Benton had managed to seduce her into secrecy with frequent raises, fat bonuses, and a per-page typing fee.

"Carolyn, keep your mouth shut and your fingers on the keyboard, okay?"

"Yes, Mr. Marsh, I understand," she'd assured him.

Clay Block rapped sharply on Benton's door.

"Come in come in, Clay."

Clay bumped into the door as he stumbled into Benton's office. Drunk again. *How does this guy manage to drive home at night?* Benton wondered. *Oh well.*

Clay sprawled in the seat in front of Marsh's desk and draped his left leg over the arm of the chair. "Uh, you wanted to see me, bossman?"

Benton frowned slightly. "Bossman" was a term Clay had started using a couple of years prior. He couldn't figure out why he disliked the sound of it. Maybe it had to do with the sarcastic tone that Clay used.

"Clay, I just got a call from a reporter in Detroit who wanted some info about Ronald Cummins."

"What did you tell him?" Clay asked.

"The usual horseshit—prolific Black crime/street corner fiction writer, etc. etc."

"They doing a piece on Cummins, huh?"

"Yeah, they're doing a piece on Cummins because he got shot to death last night in a gang-related shooting, something about a drug deal gone sour," Benton explained.

Clay slowly undraped his leg from the arm of the chair and stared at Benton's grinning face.

"So tell me, Bossman, how many unpublished manuscripts did Ronald Cummins have at Hollow Daze House when he was blown away?"

"You tell me."

"I think it was six or seven."

"Six or seven, huh? That sounds about right."

The two men reached across the desk to exchange a limp, insincere handshake.

Daddy Smooth on a Rampage began to take shape in Clay Block's head the minute he got back to his office and poured himself a drink.

"I want you to gobble up the front end of this .357 Mag, bitch!"

"Awe c'mon, Daddy Smooth, I thought I was yo' nigga."

"You *was* my nigga, punk ass bitch!"

Bam! Bam! Bam!

"Damn, Smooth, why you have to blow a hole in the motherfucker's head like that?"

"Why? I'll tell you why! When I got back here from Baghdad and found that this bitch-motherfucker-punk-ass-dog-snake had turned my sister, Ambrosia, out into them mean ass streets, I was determined to do somethin' about it."

"But, but, what about all the sisters you done turned out, Smooth?"

"That's different, this is *my* baby sister."

"So now Kenyatta's homies is gonna be comin' for yo' ass."

"I ain't afraid of them punk-ass motherfuckers! I'm armed to the teeth and should be considered highly dangerous. My question to you is this, are you with me, nigga?"

"You know I got your back, Smooth. You know that."

"Uh-oh! Look out, there's one of Kenyatta's homies over there!"

Bam! Bam! Bam!

"Did you get him?"

"I think so. Let's go over to his bleedin' body layin' out here on the street and find out."

They walk across the street, looking to their left and their right, senses wired up. They look down at the body on the street with a big .357 Mag hole in his chest. He looked up at them, dying. But before his death, he said, "You shot me, Daddy Smooth. Why did you do that? I ain't had no beef with you."

"Why did I do it? 'Cause if I didn't get you, you was gonna get me."

"For what?"

"'Cause I just shot your homie, Kenyatta."

"You killed Kenyatta? Uh-oh, yo' ass is in serious trouble now."

"Naw, it's yo' ass in serious trouble."

Bam! Bam! Bam!

"Damn, Smooth, you killed him."

"That's what usually happens when you shoot a motherfucker with a .357 Mag. Point-blank."

"So what do we do now?"

"I got some dynamite weed at my pad. Let's go get high."

"Why don't you walk in front of me. I don't wanna get my head blown off by accident."

"Why would I wanna blow your head off?"

"Well, I was just thinkin' maybe you was holdin' a grudge against me for what happened between me 'n' yo' Momma whilst you was in Baghdad."

"What happened between you and my Momma?"

Clay Block laughed aloud. This was going to be a piece o' cake. Yeah, a piece o' cake. He picked up the phone to dial his partner.

"Hey, Paul, how ya doin', baby? I got some good news. Looks like I got a li'l bit more literary impersonating to do."

"I don't feel well, Clay," Paul answered.

"Hey, what's wrong? You having the cramps on something? Ha-ha."

"No, I don't know what it is. I just don't feel well," Paul explained. "I've vomited twice today, and I'm having a little diarrhea."

"I'll be home within the hour."

Five Years Later

Alice W. Hiker-Grant and her new husband, Mel Grant, posed in front of the huge, horseshoe-shaped display of yellow roses. They had made a joint decision, backed up with a bottle of L'Authentique from Trader Joe's, to have a yellow-themed wedding on the sun deck of Mel Grant's beautiful Ladera Heights home. And after doing a bit of research, they had decided to have one of their friends perform their wedding ceremony. That's where it became somewhat tricky. The decision was riddled by a number of shared concerns.

"Oh no, we do not want any of that jumpin' over the broom shit. What's wrong with those brothers 'n' sisters?"

Alice and Mel were determined not to stand in front of a White man, no matter how many credentials he had, and have him pronounce them man and wife. And just in case there were some historically challenged individuals out there, they were prepared to point out that the Christian clergy blessed slavery—ditto for the Muslims. The couple decided that they wouldn't feel right, spiritually, to have someone from a religious persuasion that backed the African Holocaust/Diaspora perform their wedding. So then who?

They settled on Bob the bartender from the Blues Room. They had discovered that it was possible for a specific individual, on one particular, designated day to perform a wedding. It took two evenings of serious cognac drinking to convince Bob to be their "wedding man."

"Whoa! Hold on, now! I'm just a simple bartender. I ain't no preacher or nothin' like that," Bob objected.

"We know that, Bob. We also know that you were the dude who poured us the drinks that brought us together. What we're asking you to do is officiate at our wedding."

"Are you sure this is legal? I mean, I don't wanna wind up with a case or anything."

"Not a problem. Here is the way it works." They showed him the perfectly legal document that explained how an ordinary person, on one specific day, could be empowered to perform a wedding ceremony in California.

"Well I'll be damned!" Bob exclaimed. "If I had known about this, I would've had somebody marry me and Lucille. It damn sho' would've cost me less money."

Invitations were sent. Gloria, Bernice, and Coretta were designated bridesmaids. An African themed and catered banquet was planned for three hundred.

"This jollof rice is worth a marriage alone."

"How 'bout the chicken suya?"

"Alice, Mel, where did you guys get all this delicious food from?"

"Africa."

Bartender Bob, once he was completely convinced that he was going to perform a *real* wedding ceremony, really got into it.

"Now, before you two promise to love and cherish each other, keep the faith 'n' all that, before I pronounce you man and wife, I want you all to know that whenever you come to party at the Blues Room—whenever—those first two cognacs are gonna be on the house," he announced. "Now then, where were we? Oh yes, Mel Grant, do you take this lovely sister in this beautiful yellow gown to be your lawful wedded wife?"

"I do."

According to all accounts, everybody ate, drank, laughed, ate some more, drank some more, and had a damned good time. Three days later, Mr. Mel Grant and Mrs. Alice W. Hiker-Grant were on a three-week cruise to the Caribbean Island of Antigua, sipping daiquiris as they surveyed the blue-green waters of the Caribbean from their striped deck chairs.

"Alice, you've made my life complete, you know that?" Mel asked his bride.

"I could easily say the same thing."

"It's like I've spent years searching for you, not really knowing if I would find you, not really knowing if you really existed."

"And do you think I was looking for a prince in a canary-yellow suit?" Alice joked. They smiled and sipped their daiquiris.

"Incidentally, how's that going?! *The Man in the Yellow Suit*, I mean," Mel cut in.

"Well, as you know," she said, giving him a sly look, "I haven't really had a lot of time to work on it in the past few days."

The Hotel Antigua was a twenty-five room gem two-hundred yards from the beach and ocean, owned by the Davis family. "We didn't want a tourist monster hotel," the owner said. "We wanted to have a place that we would love to stay in ourselves."

Mel and Alice set up a loose schedule—a mile jog on the beach in the morning. "One of my biggest fears is that you would be one of those antiexercise intellectuals who wrote all the time," Mel admitted.

"Well, as you can see, I'm not, c'mon!" Alice responded. "I'll race you to the palm trees!"

Next, they enjoyed tea and toast with Antiguan honey for breakfast. "I had almost forgotten what honey tasted like."

Then there was their midafternoon lunch of seafood. "I could eat lobster all the time."

"We would if it were this cheap in the States."

The agenda also included late afternoon "naps" Followed by long strolls along the beach, watching the sun sink below the horizon.

"Mel Grant, did anyone ever tell you that you're a beautiful, lovin' man?" Alice asked.

"No, I guess not, because I haven't ever had anybody to be a beautiful, lovin' man to or with."

The couple enjoyed serious discussions, day and night.

"I have a few ex-girlfriends lurking around out there somewhere, but I can assure you that they are not a threat in any kind of way. And you?"

"Well, his name was Alonzo; he was twenty-four, and I was nineteen, innocent . . . . Yes, innocent and naïve."

"Meaning that he talked your panties off," Mel interjected.

"Mel, you're terrible."

"No. I'm not, remember—I was the man in the yellow suit."

They agreed on transparency in their relationship.

"You know, it's kind a funny that we would be talking about all of this kind of stuff now; I mean, after all, we've been in a relationship for a few years already."

"That was just your place/my place stuff. We weren't married then. There's a bit difference."

"Oh, I see, said the blind man."

Mel had suggestions for her about her writing career and about Hollow Daze House. "Alice, I think you oughta cut 'em loose. You know, every time you start talking about Benton Marsh, about how they put lousy covers on your books, about how they do such a lousy job of promoting your books, abut how you suspect they're cookin' the books, you look like you want to stab somebody."

"That bad, huh?" Alice asked. "It shows that much?"

"You better believe it. Look, I don't know a helluva lot about writing for a living, the publishing bizness 'n' all that, but I've heard you talk about dealing with a publisher you felt good about. Why don't you take some time when we get back to search out another publisher, first off?"

"Keep talking. I'm listening."

"You've also talked about getting an agent. I've read your works and they *are* spicy, no doubt about it, but I know there is a market for spicy works, and it doesn't have to be Horrible Hollow Daze House. Personally, I think your work is right up there with Henry Miller, Anäis Nin, D.H. Lawrence, and all the rest of 'em. The problem is that your work is always going to be considered second class so long as it's published by Hollow Daze.

"I got your back, babe. I'm making two hundred grand a year easily right now, and I won't be going into a higher tax bracket till I get past two-hundred and fifty grand, thanks to the president's tax plan, which means you don't have to be concerned about where your next lobster dinner is coming from.

"So having said that, like I said—why not scout around for another publisher, an agent?"

They enjoyed more pillow talk after a sun-blessed day doing nothing—absolutely nothing. They sprawled in the deck chairs on the balcony of their hotel room, listening to the gentle slapping of the ocean two hundred yards in front of them.

"Mel, I'm definitely going to take your advice about the publisher and agent," Alice agreed. "It may take awhile."

"You're going to be writing for the rest of your life, right?"

"God willing and the creek don't rise."

"I love those old-fashioned sayings."

"Let me ask you this—what would you like to see me write about?" Alice asked.

"Well, ha-ha, other than *The Man in the Yellow Suit*, I'd love to read a book about the African-Native American connection, romantically speaking. Why? I think it has something to do with my grandmother on my father's side being Cherokee and my grandfather on my mother's side being Choctaw.

"I don't think I've ever read anything about how these two groups connected. And obviously there was a lot of connecting. I'm not saying every African was a king and every Native American woman was a princess or vice versa, but our shared history definitely shows that we found a lot of interest in each other."

Alice W. Hiker-Grant pulled her legal pad from under her deck chair and began to scribble notes to herself; her husband smiled at her concentration.

CHAPTER 13

White on White

Ruuth Morrissey scowled at the police photographer. *You asshole you. You could've at least given me a chance to comb my hair*, she thought.

"Awright, profile shot—turn to your right. No, not that way, Ruuth, your other right."

Ruuth (*that's right, my mother insisted on spelling it with two u's; she wanted me to be different*) Morrissey slumped on one of the stone benches in the holding tank, oblivious to the funk and dirt surrounding her, a portion of her brain pan obsessed by the thought of another hit on the pipe. She tried to count backward to the last time she had had a hit. *Must be about eight hours by now*, she figured.

Writer-like, she tried to focus on the circumstances, the events that had led up to her being corralled into the police car—a casual raid on DO Squat's pad. Her present-day boyfriend, if he was still on her romantic screen, had warned her. "Ru-uth, lookahere, girl, if you gonna do bidnez with Momma Soso, don't hang out in her spot. Her place is a polease magnet."

She heard him loud and clear, but her urge to have a hit was so strong that she couldn't resist the opportunity to get high—right then and there. She shuddered at the recent memory of being caught sucking on one of Momma Soso's pipes, a piece of warped glass that Momma Soso loaned to her most dedicated customers.

"Hey, if you people want to smoke, you gotta bring your own pipes," she'd say. "I'm just sellin'—I ain't no smoke shop."

The remembered sight of the muscular men who invaded Momma Soso's place flickered in and out of her consciousness. Well, it wasn't the first time she had been busted for drug abuse . . . loitering . . . prostitution—the offense seemed a bit fuzzy in her head. *I wasn't doing prostitution. Shit, I was just trying to get enough money together to buy us a couple of hits. That's not prostitution.*

"Sid, look, I know how we can get some bread," she'd said.

"Look, Ruuth, I maybe a crackhead, but I ain't no fuckin' pimp. I don't want to see my woman out there on the corner with the rest o' them hoes. Now, whatever you do that I don't know nothin' about is another thang."

She felt something tickling up her back, leaned away from the wall to see a small circus of fleas hopping around behind. *Shit! That's all I need on my ass is a bunch of flea bites. What the fuck?* She leaned back, squirming in place to smash the fleas that had found a way through her clothes.

Looks like I might have to call on Mom and Dad this time, she thought. A wry smile crossed her face. *Who am I kidding? They wouldn't give me the center of a doughnut.*

"That's it Ruuth," her father had said. "Your mother and I have had enough of your madness. We send you to a good school, give you the best that we can give you, and what do you give us in return? Problems! Nothing but problems!"

"But Dad, what's wrong with being a writer?" Ruuth had asked.

"Maybe there's nothing wrong with being a writer, but there's a hulluva lot wrong with smoking dope all the time and having one Schwarze boyfriend after another. You have no idea how ashamed you've made me and your mother. Schwarzees! My God! Couldn't you have at least chosen one of your own kind if you were going to disgrace us?"

"I'm leaving, Dad, I'm twenty-two years old," she'd yelled. "I don't have to take this stuff any more!"

"No, you're not leaving. I'm kicking you out! And forget about coming back here! Do you understand me? You're no longer our daughter—go smoke dope with your Schwarze boyfriends! Out, out, out!"

She looked at six pairs of shoes first and then up to the three hardened faces. *Uh-oh, here we go again.*

"Get up, bitch. You sittin' on our bench," the hardest looking of the three hardened faces growled at her.

Ruuth Morrissey took a deep breath to steady her voice. She didn't want to speak in a trembling soprano. "You better git yo' Black ass outta my face, ugly bitch," she snarled.

The noises around them were suddenly muted, as though they had been lowered into the eye of a storm. The trio of toughies stared at her as though they were pit bulls getting ready to savage a piece of raw meat. The hardest looking one tried not to look shocked.

"What's that you said?"

"I didn't bite my tongue. I said, you better git yo' Black ass outta my face, ugly bitch," Ruuth repeated. "What the fuck is wrong with you? You deaf as well as ugly?"

The trio exchanged coded glances. *What the fuck do you make of this?* they silently wondered among themselves. *Who is this White bitch anyway? Now what should we do?*

Ruuth felt her heart thumping so loud she thought that anybody within five yards could hear it. She was scared shitless, but she knew she had won the first round.

She knew from bitter experience that giving in would only get her a beating and bad treatment for the rest of her time in the holding tank. Standing up to the trio might still earn her an ass kicking, but she felt they had lost the edge by hesitating to jump her. The hardest looking one probed again for weakness. "You got any cigarettes?" she asked.

"Naww, bitch, I ain't got no cigarettes." Ruuth snapped back. "What the fuck makes you think I'm supposed to be carryin' 'round cigarettes for you?"

The trio did a collective blink. She was definitely over the hump now. The hardest looking one, who looked like she had been beaten about the face with brass knuckles, softened her tone a notch.

"Hey, you don't have to be getting'all bent outta shape 'n' shit. All I did was ask you a simple fuckin' question."

"'N' all I did was give you a simple fuckin' answer."

The smallest member of the trio, a fireplug weighing at least one hundred and fifty, edged forward a step. "You one o' them smart-talkin' motherfuckers. I think I oughta kick yo' fuckin' ass!"

Ruuth took a deep breath, stood up slowly, and positioned herself like a good super middleweight—left foot forward, left fist ready to jab, right fist cocked to do a knockout. Her mother had always called her klutzy, but now, in these circumstances, being five eight and bulking one hundred and sixty-five fast food-gained pounds didn't hurt her chances of survival at all.

"You gonna kick my ass, bitch? C'mon do it," Ruuth responded.

Once again she saw the hesitation point that told her that the threat was shallow. The fireplug took a hard look at the kamikaze look in her eyes and the correct boxing stance and decided to back off. "I didn't say I was gonna kick yo' ass right now. I'll do it whenever I get ready."

"Well, bitch, whenever you get ready, I'll be ready too. Just remember that."

The leader of the trio backed away with a crooked grin on her face. "Awe, leave that bitch alone. She one o' them crazy-ass motherfuckers!"

Ruuth reached down between her legs and grabbed her crotch like a seasoned rapper.

"Yeah, that's right. I *am* one o' them crazy-ass motherfuckers! You got that right, bitch!"

They gave her a triple-layered sneer and wandered away, looking for weaker prey. Ruuth slumped back on the stone bench, shivering slightly from fear. *Bravado had worked this time, but what if they decide to get at me again?* she wondered. She wasn't completely certain she would be able to muster the necessary nerve to keep them from abusing her.

She had learned her lessons well in other episodes, in earlier confrontations, in other holding tanks around the city. A wiser, hipper, Black woman had given it to her straight up. "Up in here, in these circumstances, if you're not willin' to show that you *will* fight, your ass will be treated like dirt," she'd told Ruuth. "You know what I'm sayin'?"

Well, she had demonstrated that she was willing to fight and had fought a number of times—in fact, she had the scars from bites and scratches to prove it. But every time was new, different; she had to be ready.

She squirmed around on the bench, scratching her back against the wall to try to kill the fleas under her clothes. *Damn, I'd give anything for a hit right now.* At that moment, Ruuth looked up into the ice-blue eyes of a woman slumped on the floor five yards away from her. They mad dogged each other for a minute till Ruuth called her out. "What the fuck you starin' at, bitch?!"

The blue-eyed woman turned her eyes down and started crying softly.

Oh God, I got to get outta this place before I go nuts. Wish I had a hit, Ruuth thought.

Harvey Dawkins checked the Hollow Daze House catalogue for the third time. How in the hell could Icepick Slim and Ronald Cummins continue to have books come out of Hollow Daze House after they were long gone? He checked back through the catalogue. *Mongo's Revenge, Kenyatta's Revenge,*—lots of revenge, huh, Ron? *Bad Boyz, Ghost Killas, Murder on the Blue,* and *Cold-blooded Danny.*

He settled back in his "writing chair" to think about the situation. *Well, I guess it's each man for himself.* He had tried to communicate with each of his fellow writers—his his Hollow Daze House victims he had termed them—but never received a reply. "If you're alive, gimme some," he had e-mailed. And he never received a reply. *Oh well.*

Why in the fuck should I be concerned about these goofy-ass motherfuckers? I swam up from the bottom of the barrel. It took the pause of a blink to remind him of whatever he came from, the bittersweet basements of Chicago's Westside, before it was "regentrified"—what it felt like to live in a hotel/brothel on the south side of the ghetto.

"C'mere, li'l boy, lemme suck yo' dick," he remembered one woman saying. "You evah had anybody suck yo' dick befo'?"

"No ma'am," he'd responded meekly.

Harvey did a mental review of what he had released to Hollow Daze House Publishing Company. Amazingly, they had published *Time Out,* which was his signature ghetto fiction crime scene novel. Why?

Harvey laced his hands behind his head, thinking hard on the years that had made him a "best-selling author" within the Hollow

Daze House pantheon. Unlike some of the other Hollow Daze people, he had done a little homework and discovered that Hollow Daze House sold a fair share of books within the pulp book market, and maybe more because they had closed in on the African American pulp fiction market, on the West Coast at any rate.

The biggest market was behind bars. He was surprised to receive so many fan letters from San Quentin, Chino, Folsom, Vacaville, and Lompoc and a few from other prisons from around the country.

Well, if nothing else, that tells me that I have a captive audience anyway, he thought. *Time to stop the wool gathering.* He leaned back over to make a few notes on his outline for his next novel, tentatively titled *Hollow Daze.* Bet Benton would have me assassinated if he knew I was writing about him and that crooked bullshit he's doing.

Clay Block emptied his lover's bedpan, washed it out in the toilet sink, and returned to the bedroom where Paul laid in bed, reed thin, hollow-eyed, and feverish.

"Clay, sweetheart," Paul whispered as Clay sat in the chair at the bedside.

"Yes, Paul, I'm here."

It took him a few moments to gather the strength to speak. "I want you to know that I love you."

"And I love you too, Paul."

Clay Block gently scooped his partner up into his arms and held him. *In spite of all the medicines, he's dying,* Clay silently mourned. *And I'm sick.* It had not surprised him to discover that he was HIV positive.

"Sorry to have to tell you this, Mr. Block, but your test came back positive," the doctor had reported.

"I thought it would, Doc."

"Sorry."

Clay was feeling sick but not despondent. *There's no time to be down,* he said to himself. *I have to take care of Paul.*

Jack Mozel felt like thousands of insects were crawling all over his body. He felt like the walls of his cell were throbbing, that they were opening and closing on his head. He was screaming hysterically, but he couldn't connect himself to the screams.

Why doesn't that guy stop screaming so that I can get some rest? Jack thought.

The claustrophobia had been building for a long time. Early on he had used all of the self-control he could muster to deny the claustrophobia any traction. He had focused on the Gothic-shaped glass window slitted in the door of his cell, pretending that the window opened up on a view of the ocean, of the wide-open spaces of the desert. But the window didn't offer a view of any of those things.

He stood at the window hour after hour, staring at the cells across from him. Occasionally, two faces would appear in the slits on the other side of the corridor. The faces were contorted, ugly, mean looking, both insane from the crazy stuff in their brains and from being alone for almost twenty-three hours a day.

Jack managed to bear the pressure of his cell during the daytime; after all, the guards strolled past, and food was pushed through the slot in the door of his cell. The pressure became unbearable at night when no one came to look into his cell, and no one came to push food through the slot in the door. Some nights seemed to last for weeks.

From the very beginning, Jack had thought of hundreds of little tricks to try to cope with the claustrophobia, the loneliness, and the loss of freedom of movement. He wrote stories in his head, he did push-ups and sit-ups till he collapsed, he tried to imagine that he was somewhere else. He felt that he was doing well, coping, till the realization hit him that he was going to have to cope with his circumstances for the rest of his life. And he had only been in prison for three months.

He began to slowly crumble inside after the reality of where he was and what was facing him sank in. He screamed for hours on end, his lungs suddenly lead-lined from anger, fear, craziness. And there were other times when he felt the weight of Ron Wildstock's head in his arms, times when he heard the snap-crack of Wildstock's neck over and over.

He stopped screaming long enough to turn his back to the slitted window and bite into the back of his wrists. The blood that flowed out tasted salty, much spicier than the food he was given to eat every day. He bit harder and harder.

Anything would be better than rotting away in this cell—anything. He woke up in the hospital, handcuffed and foot shackled to the hospital bed. He smiled at the quiet activity going on around him, the doctor and the nurses going from one shackled patient to another. *My turn*, he thought.

"Well now, young fella," the doctor said, "looks like you're trying to cause yourself a big problem."

"No problem, Doc, just tryin' to save the tax payers a little money."

The doctor looked up from a close study of his chart, frowned, and whispered to the guard at his side.

"I'd keep this one on suicide watch for a while."

The guard nodded in agreement. They moved on to the next man. Jack Mozel stared up at the lightbulb above his head. The lightbulb was enclosed by a wire grill. *Damn, everything here is behind bars, even the light bulb.*

The scream that erupted from his body sent chills up to the spines of all the people on the ward. The doctor called to his head nurse. "Nurse, please prepare a sedative for that man." And then he turned to whisper to the guard. "I'm afraid he's lost it. I've seen it before. He has decided that life is not worth living, and he'll do whatever he can to kill himself."

"We'll do the best we can to prevent it," the guard said grimly.

"Good luck."

CHAPTER 14

All's Well That Ends . . .

Benton Marsh drummed his fingers on the edge of his neatly arranged, uncluttered desk. He checked his watch. *He'll be on time, I'd make book on it.* He had another meeting with Harvey Dawkins.

This little bastard has been complaining about something since day one. Now what? Benton wondered. *There's no need to try to prepare my head for what he might be bringing me.*

Benton leaned back in his chair, tented his fingers under his chin, and did a flash drive review of his twenty-some-year-old back-and-forth with Dawkins. *Damn, we've crossed a lot of bridges together, not holding hands or doing anything warm and fuzzy, but history is a fact, someone once said.*

My partner, Ron, gone. My son, the dope fiend, gone.

"Dad, can you send me five hundred dollars? I'm stuck down here in a little flea-bitten town in Mexico."

"No, I will not send you five hundred dollars to support your drug habit." Gone, somewhere, God only knows where.

Clay Block, the best and drunkest editor I ever had. That guy made me a lot of money with his Icepick Slim and Ronald Cummins books. Too bad about him and his boyfriend. Gone.

Then there was Ruuth Morrissey. "Benton," she'd said, "I've just written one of my best novels ever. I call it *In the Tank.* Can I drop it off tomorrow? You'll love it."

"Uh, sure, Ruuth, let's say about ten or so."

"See ya."

The odor she brought into his office and her appearance when she arrived shocked him. She looked as though she had been sleeping in grease spots underneath cars. Another junkie. What's the deal with these middle-class White kids who want to live the lousy life? *In the Tank* was so bad he could barely stumble through the first ten pages. And the manuscript couldn't be returned to her, because the address she gave him was nonexistent. Gone.

Hell, whose left? he thought to himself. The phone on his desk rang.

"Yeah, Carolyn?"

"Mr. Dawkins is here to see you."

"Send him in."

Who was left? Me and this little prick, Dawkins. Benton couldn't resist a little smile watching Harvey Dawkins pop through the door. This guy always looked like he just popped out of a popcorn cooker or something. Dawkins leaned across Benton's desk for the limp handshake they managed to exchange each time they had a meeting.

"So what do you have to complain about this time, Harvey Dawkins?" Benton began.

Harvey's eyes narrowed to slits. *You motherfucker you. Well, I guess this is as good a way as any to drop off into this shit.* "Benton, you're weird, man, you know that? Every time I meet with you, you seem to think that I'm here to pinch your balls or something."

Benton settled back in his chair. He knew it was senseless to invite Harvey to sit in the seat in front of his desk. Obviously Harvey enjoyed pacing back and forth.

"So why are you here, Harvey?" Benton questioned.

Harvey took a position to the left side of Benton's desk, crossed his arms, and stood in place, staring into Benton's puzzled eyes for a few moments. He wasn't going to go away soon; Benton could see that from the solid planting of his feet.

"Let's start with my missing royalties from the past two quarters."

"Didn't you get your statement?"

Harvey shook his head in disbelief. *Oh God, don't tell me this ol' motherfucker is gonna go* there? *How many times over the years, whenever royalty checks came up missing, did he say, "Didn't you get your statement?"*

"Okay, Benton, you want to play that little game, huh? Well, not today, I don't have time for it. This is about something much more serious."

Harvey took note of the look of fake innocence that washed over Benton's face. It was if Benton was silently saying, *I see no evil, hear no evil, speak no evil. And I don't know anything.* Harvey felt like laughing. How could this evil ol' bastard put on such an innocent face?

"My goodness gracious, Harvey, you really look serious. What's the problem? You wanna talk about it?"

"That's what I came to do, Benton, that's what I came to do," Harvey confirmed.

"Well, let it out already."

Harvey Dawkins took a deep breath. *Now I know why Jack Mozel broke Ron Wildstock's neck. Be cool, be cool man. Losing your temper is not the thing to do.*

"I've just discovered, much to *my* surprise, that you no longer own Hollow Daze House Publishing Company . . . that you had an assets sale to Kingston Press, which includes my books. What that means is that you are no longer selling my books, and Kingston doesn't have me in its current catalogue or on its website," Harvey explained. "In other words, I'm in limbo. I've been hung out to dry."

"Harvey, I hope you didn't come here to try to tell me how to run my business."

The statement stunned Harvey and stopped him from pacing back and forth. Logically, one section of his brain said, *Of course I can't tell you how to run your business.* But the emotional side wanted to scream, *You should've had the decency to tell me that my shit had been sold to somebody else. It's not about obligation, you prick. It's about common courtesy.*

"Okay, Benton, you got that right," Harvey agreed. "I can't tell you how to run your business, but as one of your 'best selling' authors, it seems to me that you would've had the courtesy to call me and tell me that my titles were being sold."

"Didn't you get a call from Carolyn? I told her to call you."

Harvey felt like screaming. *Nobody called me to tell me a goddamned thing. If I hadn't gotten antsy after two full quarters and called your receptionist to find out what was happening, I would still be in the dark.*

"Oh, Harvey, didn't Mr. Marsh call you to tell you that he had sold Hollow Daze to Kingston?—They're layin' me off."

"Uh, no, Benton, nobody called me to tell me shit."

"Huff! I thought I told Carolyn to call you about the sale," Benton said.

The two men stared at each other. Benton felt comfortable with his lie, and Harvey felt an impotent rage about the whole situation. He knew, legally, that he didn't have a brief, but he decided to try to lean on Benton a bit.

"Well, no matter what happens, I want the rights to my books," Harvey finally said, breaking the silence.

"Harvey, my friend," Benton spoke in his suavest fake voice, "I have nothing to do with any of that. You'll have to deal with Kingston about those matters."

Harvey Dawkins, not completely unaware of the dark sides of the publishing business, thought quickly about the job of going up against a multimillion-dollar empire to retrieve the rights to the books that Hollow Daze House and Benton Marsh had sold.

"So I guess that means that I won't have to see your ol' ugly ass again, huh?"

"Not unless you wanna do lunch sometime?"

Harvey was tempted to laugh aloud. What could you say that would be insulting to Benton? Apparently nothing.

Benton Marsh laid his clothes out for the next day across the back of his bedside chair. He leaned forward and felt the sudden pangs of pain in both hips. *Damn! This arthritis is getting worse all the time.*

He placed both hands on his hips, trying to squeeze off the pain. This was going to be a two-Ibuprofen night; he could literally feel it in his bones. He shuffled into the bathroom and poured a couple of pills into his left hand. He popped them into his mouth and took a swig from a glass of water. That done, he removed his dentures and sank them into a glass of warm water.

He gripped the edge of the marbled toilet sink and slowly looked up at the wrinkled, toothless figure with the receding hairline. *So you're old. Well, everybody gets old.* He thought about telling himself a joke about being old but dismissed the thought. Who the hell wants to be old? Specially if you're in some kind of pain all the time: arthritis, ulcers, migraines, hearing problems, high blood pressure, prostate—*I thought only Blacks had that kind of problem*—gout, skin cancers on the nose and cheeks, constipation, impotence. *Well, that's no problem. Sarah's been dead for years now, and so have I. Who needs a stiff prick when you don't have a wife?*

He shuffled back to his bedroom—huge bedroom, big house, lots of rooms, Bel Air, an exclusive section of well-heeled Los Angeles. He made a mental note to remind his Mexican maid, Señora Suarez, to clean the gunky corners of his bedroom again.

It was November in southern California and pleasantly cool at night. He buttoned the neck of his cotton pajamas and slid in under a puffy blanket, searched around for the television remote, surfed for a few minutes, and decided not to spend time listening to or looking at Leno/Letterman.

It's all a bunch of subliminal conditioning, he thought. *You'd be a fool not to understand that. It's all a bunch of bullshit.*

He nodded off, forgetting to click off his beside lamp. A half hour later, as though he were awakening from a gentle nightmare, he stared into the soft glow of the lamp. He cradled his hands behind his head.

"Benton, you know something, if you were one of my hoes, I would force your ass to get out there and turn tricks till you got my money right."

"Unfortunately for you, Icepick, I'm not one of your hoes."

A face-off with Icepick Slim. God, did I actually do that?

"Look, Benton, I'm ghetto. Shall I say more?" Ronald Cummins, dope fiend writer, had said. *Thanks, Clay, I think you did the guy a favor by fleshing out his career.*

Jack Mozel—you beast-monster! Why didn't you shoot Ron? Why did you have to break his neck? Well, what the hell does it matter? You've twisted yourself into a life sentence. Here's looking at you, kid!

Benton wiped the corners of his eyes. *Ron Wildstock was an asshole and a racist bastard, but he was my asshole and my racist bastard. Otherwise, he was a good guy.*

Ruuth Morrissey had once told him, "I'm not trying to prove anything, and I don't have to." *Sorry, Ruuthie, you had a lot to prove, and Hollow Daze House helped you. Sure, we made money, but that's what businessmen are supposed to do. Too bad your identity crisis was responsible for you slipping into crack and then down through the cracks. C'est la vie.*

Alice W. Hiker-Grant's beige-colored face and bright, sarcastic smile swam just past his consciousness. "Benton," she's said, "you've got to understand—if you possess that capacity—that I'm *not* embarrassed about being published by Hollow Daze, but I do know that I won't be with you after this book. I'm moving onward, upward."

Benton crossed and recrossed his legs, agitated by his sound-bite thoughts. *What the hell could these people bitch and complain about? If it hadn't been for Hollow Daze, they wouldn't've been published at all.*

Harvey Dawkins. Benton Marsh took a deep breath—just the way the last therapist had told him to do—closed his eyes, and tried to blot out the memory of Harvey Dawkins. Bastard.

"Listen to me, Benton, 'cause I'm not goin' to repeat myself. I don't have absolute proof right now, but I'm gonna dig for it, about how Hollow Daze has ripped us off.

"I've asked the Authors Guild and the National Writers Union to help me bring a suit against you to find out where the bones are buried. I know that you've had somebody write books for Icepick and Ronald Cummins. I feel that in my bones. I'm comin' for you, Benton."

Benton Marsh smiled up at the expensive light fixture in the ceiling. *Sorry, Harvey, you're blowing smoke up your own butt. I've covered my tracks so well you'd have to resurrect Clay Block to get what you want. And you would have to be a magician to find the recipe for all the books I've cooked. Of course I cheated you and all of the people who came through Hollow Daze House, but that's the nature of the business.*

Benton unlaced his hands from behind his head and laid them across his chest. *That's the nature of the business. Who doesn't know that?*

CHAPTER 15

Bye Bye Babysweets

Señora Suarez rang the doorbell a dozen times.

Guess the ol' fart is sleeping late. It was nine o'clock in the morning. He was usually up for his coffee by now. She checked out the car in the drive way, puzzled. *He must be here; his car is here*, she thought. She walked around the rear of the large, fake Tudor building. No open door there. She called on her cell and left a message. "Meester Marsh, this is Sarafina Suarez, the housekeeper. I am outside waiting—come to open the door. I have work to do."

There was nothing she could do but wait for him to get up. She went back to sit on the front steps. This was very unusual, Mr. Marsh usually met her at the front door, anxious to extract as much labor out of her as possible. She worked from nine to six thirty Monday through Wednesday and Friday.

The Bel Air police drove by, waved cordially at the maid camped out on the front steps, circled the five-mile perimeter of their district, and drove back. People didn't like to have the help hanging around.

"What's the problem, Sarafina? Mr. Marsh won't let you in?" the officer asked.

She shrugged eloquently. "I don't know what the problem is with him," she said.

Officer Swanson made a station call to let his dispatcher know that he had stopped to "help a maid in distress."

"Let's see what's going on here." Officer Swanson rang the front doorbell a few times and marched to the rear of the house, trailed by Señora Suarez. He peeked through the back windows, then the side windows.

"Meester Marsh, he always opens the door for me."

Officer Swanson took careful note of the fact that there were no tracks underneath the windows, no visible signs of burglary. And the old guy's car was still in the driveway.

Maybe he's fallen and fractured a hip or something. Officer Swanson called his duty station. "Badge 682 calling. I'm at 301 Ocean View Drive, the home of Mr. Benton Marsh. We may have an emergency situation here. I'm requesting permission to make a forced entry."

"Sergeant Bradford will be there within ten minutes," dispatch responded. "Do not take any action until he arrives."

Sergeant Bradford was on the scene within five minutes. The Bel Air police were well paid and took great pride in their reputation for efficiency.

"What seems to be the trouble, Phil?"

"Well, Sarafina here, the maid, can't get in, and I've taken a look around . . . . Doesn't look like a burglary scene or anything like that. Mr. Marsh's car is in the driveway, I'm thinking he may have had a fall and broken something."

"That's possible. Okay, permission to make a forced entry is granted. We can do the paperwork later."

The officers used a miniature ramrod to pound the back door open and entered cautiously.

"Mr. Marsh, you in here, sir?" No response.

They walked through the spacious rooms on the first floor and continued calling out. "Mr. Marsh?"

"Meester Marsh—he sleeps upstairs."

She led the two policemen up the carpeted stairs that she had vacuumed many times. Señora Suarez stood in the door of Benton's bedroom and crossed herself. The grim, tortured expression on his face told her that the old man was dead. She had seen enough dead people in the Narco wars of her native city, Culiacan, to recognize the terribly still look of death.

While the two policemen made a careful study of the scene and of Benton Marsh, Señora Sarafina Suarez frowned and cursed under her breath. "You ol', stingy bastard. Why did you have to die the day before my payday?"

True to his word, Harvey Dawkins continued his efforts to obtain a reversion of the rights to his books and finally succeeded after a year. He was also able to find out, to his satisfaction, that a number of books credited to Icepick Slim and Ronald Cummins had been written by the deceased editor, Clay Block.

"Look, Carolyn, this won't get you into any legal problems at all."

"Well, like I said, I just did the typing. Clay Block created the books, and all I did was type them," she finally explained. "Block was almost a genius. It was like he could write in the other person's style real easy. So what happens now? I mean, Mr. Marsh is dead, Block is dead, Icepick and Cummins too."

"What happens now? Now we know that Benton Marsh was responsible for creating false products. I'm pretty sure that there are some other skeletons in the closet, stuff like cheating on our royalties," Harvey said.

"I don't know anything about that."

"I'm sure you don't, but I bet somebody else does, and when I find that person, or persons, I'm going to gather up as many of the family members of the writers who've been cheated, had the books cooked on them, and file a class-action suit against Benton Marsh's estate."

"Wow!" Carolyn gasped. "You're serious, huh?"

"As serious as a pit bull on a steak bone."

More

The class-action suit by the family members of the writers is currently in litigation, and their prospects of receiving justice seem to be good. It all depends on which way the dice roll.